VIOLIN

Son of an Abuser

A NOVEL

Tahiti Marie Press

Also by Jude Emmanuel

I Heard Xavier Cry

A Decision Made with Love

VIOLIN

Son of an Abuser

A NOVEL

JUDE EMMANUEL

Violin: Son of an Abuser is a work of fiction. Names, characters, places, and incidents, either are the product of the author's imagination or are used fictitiously. Any resemblance to actual persons, living or dead, events, or locales, is entirely coincidental.

In memory of *Tatoune,*
the gracious woman who gave me life.

ACKNOWLEDGEMENTS

A peculiar thing happened right after completing this novel. Though I will forever be thankful to many; it was never my intention to bestow recognition to anyone on such page. But then, I couldn't resist sharing a little bit about an odd twist of fate. In doing so, I harken back to the first novel I had ever read: *Madame Bovary*, by the renowned French writer, Gustave Flaubert. I don't know what prompted me to read it at the time, but I did. I was about to turn twelve years old when I first read it. While I had somewhat of a difficult time fully understanding what the novel was about, flipping through its pages, I nonetheless, appreciated the mastery and elegance of its prose. It unearthed a new world for me. Even at such a young age, the world of literature had enticed me. It captured my imagination and made itself my first love. I had not thought about that novel in over decades. And so, since I was going to reference *Madame Bovary*, I decided to look back and browsed through what exactly was so captivating. Only to discover the strange symmetry in "literary realism" in reference to this novel. It remains a mystery to me. It amazed me to find out, after it was published, *Madame Bovary* was viewed as "taboo" by many. In no way am I comparing my work to that of a literary genius. But with *Son of an Abuser* as a subtitle, to some, it may spell fireworks. Whether my mind had been cultivated by an eccentric literature, someone else can be the judge. Nevertheless, literature is not just about art. It's about life, when the toxic breaths one inhales desperately want to come out. I pay homage to Gustave, as well as countless others, who have opened my heart to the world of literature. Along the road, there has been the discovery of life inspiring creative minds, past and contemporary, whom I am indebted to for life. Thank you all for opening my heart to the wonderful world of literature.

CONTENTS

INTRODUCTION

Growing up, he was always thoughtful, yet withdrawn. As reclusive as he was, he had been taking it all in. He discovered there were two sides to love, undying affection and jealous rage. Love had always been bittersweet. It had always been like a sting in the tail or like elderberry twigs. "Even roses have thorns," his mother says to him. Anguish taught him just as much about life as love did. To him, walking through life was like having a shrub of African violet planted on one foot, and a damper of English ivy on the other. Though he tried, could a young man really escape the sins of the predator, when the demons' spheres already lived within. "Like father, like son," is the way great tales of father and son stories are told. Not to this son. He strove to be more like his mother. Yet, no matter how much he fought them, his demons played like a symphony in his soul.

And so, long ago, in a small island in the Caribbean, life was full of promise for his parents, a young couple with three children. Even though they were able to provide for their children, the couple wasn't well-off. Their dream was to travel to America; the United States of America that is. Everybody wanted to come to America back then. I suppose many still do, vying to come to America. To them, it indeed is the land of the free and home of the brave. Nevertheless, when migrating to the land of the brave, one must not forget to take your bravery with you. If life was full of promise then for the young couple, surely, coming to America would entice them even more with the hope of the great *American Dream*. They were known as the Labonnes, the "good family" as they were often called back home. Yet, there was nothing honorable about the horror each one was going to face in America. "Welcome to America," the mother says to her youngest son, when they lastly reunited after many years. While their tragic story happened to take place in a foreign land, this was not solely about America. The dismay of life, tormenting many souls, exists throughout the world: Poverty, crime, lawlessness, and even demons. Not the ones seen on the screen masquerading as cartoon like characters. But the ones in us. The inner struggles persecuting our minds. Those are the ones to fear. They lie in wait, until they explode with the fury of a wildfire. Even then, we tend to ignore them, until it is too late. However, the damages they inflict upon us are as real as can be. Though it might have been the last thing they expected; the remnant of a violent storm had landed with the couple and their children in America. It had followed them like the wind of a hurricane.

They were, was his luthier

They didn't use a bow,

just plucked his delicate strings

He couldn't bear

He has the highest voice

Only some can comprehend

He was different

One, couldn't devote

Two, would rejoice

Three, shouldn't assume,

while using a head voice

He was pretending, causing so many to neglect

And yet, it reflected

They heard his cry; yet couldn't understand

Obscure

Domestic violence, envious mayhem!

-S. Deslouches

CHAPTER ONE

I was never interested in words, until I had to put my thoughts to paper. And when I did, I despised what I saw. Before I could get a chance to erase it, the ink had dried out. I ripped up the paper, tearing it to pieces. But my eyes had already seen the pain. It was like looking into a mirror. You don't forget the scars on your face simply because you walk away. They stay with you. They're in your head. Just as the menacing thoughts have been engraved in my memory. I'm married, but I don't really have a family. My wife left me. The one I truly loved. The other ones, I didn't care for as much. Or perhaps I did; I did love again. After the one I truly loved left me. That's assuming I still know what love is. I don't know anymore. Life is just passing me by. I'm worthless, cursing my life. Half hour past midnight, nothing has changed. Everything will be the same tomorrow and the next day. I have four children, three girls, and one boy. They all hate me. Or perhaps not. They say they don't. I've learned, the heart can change on a whim. Why am I here, between these four walls? I did everything right, I thought. Why did hell and I cross paths?

Brooklyn, New York, that's where my road to hell began. I was only thirteen years old then.

"Help me, Violin. Please! He's beating the hell out of me."

I'm so scared. My heart is racing. I don't know what to do.

"Daddy! Please stop."

Patches of her hair arc on the floor like autumn leaves.

"Shut the hell up, you stupid slut." He has her by the throat again.

"Oh my God! Please, Daddy, Stop. You're going to kill her!"

She's gasping for air. She can't breathe.

"Run Mommy! Run!"

It was all a dream. She's gone. She's dead now. Her scars still live with me. Her misery didn't die with her.

It left her body when she went six feet under. Her sorrows are now with me. I don't know where she is. But she sure *ain't* with me. I'm left to carry her anguish alone. Life isn't fair; I tell whoever cares to listen. They don't hear me. No one cares. She's in Heaven they say. So What? I'm here suffering all alone. Who cares enough to listen to me anyway? No one cares what I have to say. I'll die soon. No one will remember me. I'm dying a slow death, one breath at a time. Nobody sees it. I have had to bury too much inside ever since I was little. I'm still a young boy, but I feel as though I'm eighteen or maybe twenty-five. Yes! Twenty-five years old. Then, I can walk into a bar, order a drink, meet a beautiful girl, and get married. I'll have lots of children then. Or maybe not. No children for me. I'm too scared; afraid I will hurt them like Daddy hurt me. I'm only thirteen, but my mind tells me I'm older. Life wasn't supposed to be this way Mamma said, but it is.

I told Mamma, when I get married, I sure as hell didn't want to be like Daddy. I had hoped that my brother would be different. But he's just like Daddy. They have the same roots. He beats up on his wife and kids, then says he's sorry. Sometimes, sorry isn't enough. As for my sister, her man beats up on her too. That's crazy; they're not even married. I told her to leave him. Leave that woman beater alone, I tell her. She won't do it. She won't listen to me. She's in love, she says. I'm just a little boy; why should she listen to me. I knew long ago she was hiding sin; after she lied to Mamma about her black eye. "Sit your black hinny down, and stop worrying about grownup business," she says. I hate it when she calls me *that*. It cuts inside my ribs like a chainsaw. I crack a smile so my teeth don't gnash. Since when being Black was a curse? And I sure as hell a*in't* no donkey. I may not know much about grown folks' stuff; my face may not show it, still I laugh. At least I'm old enough not to let no other man beat me. Except for Daddy, of course. It used to be the four of us in the house with him; now it's just me. I hate him, but I love him. He's my daddy. Mamma often said the same thing. She hates him, but she loves him. I miss Mamma. She was a beautiful lady. I miss her home cooked meals. She made breakfast every morning before leaving for work. Once, she cooked a whole week with her hand wrapped in a cast. I can still smell her cooking. Sometimes I wake up with the whiff of her scrambled eggs all over my room. Even the awful stench of the herbal cocktail she called medicine. Her sweet raisin pancakes tasted like honey from heaven.

Mamma is now in Heaven. They say it is where kindhearted people go. She was a good woman. I hope she's not looking down at me. I let her down. My heart is filled with so much guilt. She must think I'm a disgrace for a son. Mamma was always nice to me. I let her down. She was already gone, I thought; someone had to protect Daddy. I cried so much at her funeral; my shirt was soaked with tears. I was crying for her and for Daddy. I cried a lot for me too. I was afraid to look down at the casket. Mamma looked upset. Maybe she was mad at me. My hands were just as drenched with her blood. Though I was innocent. It took a lot of grown men, strong muscular men, to pull Josie away from Mamma's casket. "I'm so sorry I left, Mamma," she kept crying. She wanted Mamma to come back. Although she kept screaming, the music never stopped. The choir continued to give praise, and the pastor seemed oblivious to her frantic shouts. Everyone appeared to have turned a deaf ear to our cries. It wasn't such a surprise. It was what they had always done. It must have been the loneliest sobs Josie had ever felt. Jessy, as well, struggled to keep it all in. As Mamma's first born, he was holding his anger from boiling over. The way his head started to shake, I knew it was only a matter of time before he let loose his guilt. "Hmmm, Mamma, I'm so sorry you're gone; Hmmm, Mamma please forgive me," he started humming. His body twirled like a castoff serpent on the ground. My heart sank with grief. There were so many people at the funeral home that day. Death had welcomed Mamma with a dozen circle of friends. They were all hypocrites, crying hysterically and falling. "Violine,

Violine," they all bellowed out, shouting enough tears to make up for a lifetime of neglect. They might as well had been pretending. Their bodies quivered, as if dancing for joy. Where were they when Mamma needed them? It was my first time seeing them ever. "We are all family," they said. It stirred my blood. They all had left us for dead. Like the night when hell took over our home. Daddy was so upset; he started hitting everyone in the house. Mamma worried a lot about me. She thought I was going to die. Daddy kicked me so hard, the wall around me started to crack. My whole body was hurting. It felt as if my bones were about to break. That night, Daddy threw all four of us out of the house. We waited all night at the bottom of the steps for someone to pick us up. One of her brothers or sisters, Mamma said, would come for us. None of them showed up. We all slept on the floor in the hallway outside our apartment. Apartment 5H, I remember it to this day. I had stared at it for most of the night before falling asleep. Even then, I thought the "H" stood for hell. But Mamma said the number five was the number of grace—God's grace. They were the same to me, hell, and grace. Our hell was also our grace. Daddy took care of us and at the same time hated us.

Mamma had to call for help from a neighbor's phone. We waited all night. No one showed up. It was my first time seeing the horror Mamma told me about. I don't know what "Hell" looks like, but it felt like it. We were in it—all of us—me, Mamma, my older brother and my sister. Mamma said she lost her dignity that night. She'd lost it a long time ago, I reckoned. She said it was because it happened in front of us. Her children had finally seen with their own eyes what her hell was like. She always said her life wasn't pretty. I saw the ugly truth in her broken nose. It was a half hour past midnight when it happened. There was nowhere else for us to go. The old lady next door said we could use her phone, but she couldn't offer us a place to sleep. Mamma wasn't mad at her. The old lady didn't want to get involved. No one did, not even Mamma's brothers and sisters. What did she have them for? I thought. Perhaps we didn't get any help because we were immigrants. It was our first time visiting the United States—me, Jessy, and Josie. We had only been in the U.S. a couple of days. We had left home to be with Mamma. We used to live with Aunt Clarissa back home before Daddy finally agreed for us to come. Mamma told him she was lonely without her children. She was thinking about moving back home if Daddy insisted, we couldn't come. Daddy caved in. Then again, he may have regretted doing so. Three days after arriving in Brooklyn, we were all sleeping on a cold mosaic floor outside of our own home. It was really Daddy's house. That's what he kept telling

7

Mamma. "All of you, get out my house," he kept on yelling. But it wasn't a house; not like the one we lived in back home. When I first got there, I thought we were moving in a warehouse. I didn't care, as long as I was going to be with Mamma. It was a scary looking building, with a bunch of young men smoking funny smelling cigars in the lobby. At least that's what I thought it was at the time. There were graffiti all over the walls. At first, I started to think it was a poorly painted building, until I saw one of my favorite hip hop artist's name written on the wall. We used to listen to him on the radio back home. Even then, as it was still in its beginning years, hip hop was a powerful beast. It invaded the souls of so many, back home. Perhaps it was worshipped because it was the type of music that gave young men and women hope.

It was early fall of 1982. As we later found out, Brooklyn was not for the faint of heart. We could hear the train running all night. It was almost pitch-black in the hallway outside the apartment. The ceiling light had apparently been broken for a while. Back home, somebody would have helped. Now that we were in a foreign land, no one seemed to care, not our neighbors, not even our own family. "Welcome to America," Jessy quipped, as we all lay on the floor. It was how Mamma greeted us at the airport. Jessy always had a fresh mouth. Mamma didn't say much. Maybe she felt too humiliated to utter a word. We piled on top of one another like desolate refugees, near the dark stairs. I was too terrified to say anything. Too angry for the right words to come out without adding to Mamma's misery.

"You all right, *Cheri*?" she asked. It was her way of calling me sweetheart. I started to laugh, hoping my tears would not show. "Bonne nuit," I said, restraining a rush of more tears. It was never going to be a good night, not ever. Not after what I had seeing Mamma go through that night. Her tears had the color of blood. The next morning, when he was leaving for work, Daddy told all of us to go back inside. Mamma's eyes were still pink like the gloomy sky. She was still shedding tears. She had me put a bandage over the gaping cut above her right eye. Her nose was still bleeding. She wasn't crying because of her wounds. Her heart was broken. She cried throughout the night. Every time I got up, I would hear her sobbing and praying to God. "Oh Jesus!" she wept. Mamma was tired.

It was my first-time seeing Daddy beat on Mamma. It didn't feel right, seeing him dragging her by the hair like a roping horse. Mamma told me about him beating her all the time. I imagined what it was like. The skylark screamed just as loudly in my ears. When we were back home, Mamma would call in the middle of the night. "You better not kill my sister," Aunt Clarissa told Daddy. He held a knife to Mamma's throat, threatening to kill her. Daddy always did that. I wouldn't go to sleep; not until we had heard from Mamma. I would wait for her to call; praying she was still alive. Three, four, sometimes every single night of the week, Mamma called. I lay in bed crying. Most nights, even after hearing her voice, it was still hard for me to fall asleep. What if something happened while my eyes were closed? I fought my sleep. That's how I kept Mamma alive. As long I could picture her in my head; I knew she was still breathing. One night, I swore she was dead. I had spent all day at school thinking about her. There was this aching in my stomach, telling me something bad was going to happen.

"Why are you not sleeping? Go to bed," Aunt Clarissa shouted at me.

"I'm waiting for Mamma to call," I told her. Aunt Clarissa didn't like when I talked back. But this time, she wasn't upset that I did.

"It's midnight, please go to sleep," she said.

"I'm waiting for Mamma to call," I once again told her. Though she didn't say it, she also was waiting for Mamma to call. She was pacing back and forth and had a worried look on her face. So, we both waited.

The phone rang. "Hello," I answered, after Aunt Clarissa told me to pick it up. It was Mamma.

"Oh Lord Jesus! Call an ambulance," she shouted, "my son picked up the phone."

Although Mamma was very upset with Aunt Clarissa for allowing me to pick up the phone, it may have saved her life. She was bleeding a whole lot. Mamma wanted to leave life. After hearing my voice, she held on, wanting to live again. That's when I came up with my plan. Mamma needed my help. I asked God to forgive me. I would have to tell a big lie. Only Uncle Ronald knew about it. Daddy liked him a lot. I told Uncle Ronald to tell Daddy we needed to come up, because Mamma was planning on getting on a plane without Daddy knowing to come to us. And If Daddy still didn't want us to come, I told Uncle Ronald to tell him someone had threatened to kidnap me. While it didn't happen that often, a little girl on our block had been abducted the month before. They wanted a lot of money to bring her back. Her parents couldn't afford to pay. So, the abductors never brought her back. Six months later, Aunt Clarissa told me we were going to America to live with our parents. I felt bad about leaving Aunt Clarissa behind, but I needed to be with Mamma. My brother and sister were ecstatic. They couldn't believe it. They were in shock when I later told them what I had done. "I did it for Mamma," I told Jessy and Josie. They were much older than me. Jessy was seventeen, and my sister, Josie, fifteen. Uncle Ronald thought I was a lot smarter. "I know you're just a little boy," he said, "But when you go up there now, make sure you take care of your mother." I loved Uncle Ronald. He was my only uncle on my father's side of the family. He was the only one Daddy ever listened to.

And so, the night Daddy started beating all four of us, he somehow must've found out what I had done. Uncle Ronald had told Mamma what to say to Daddy; so he could agree to allow us to come. Perhaps Daddy heard me talking to Mamma about it. He was enraged. "For you to conspire against your own father, there's no way you can be my son," he growled at me. No wonder he had kicked me so hard. Still, he thought we all had plotted against him. Jessy and Josie got a few punches on the back. But Mamma and I, we were like kicking bags at a martial arts' gym. Daddy most likely assumed she and I were the masterminds behind the secret plan. Mamma wasn't to blame. It was me; I'm the one who told Uncle Ronald about the plan. I felt guilty and afraid. I was so scared Daddy would send me back. Although he didn't, he said we all had to follow his rules. I felt heartbroken for Mamma. She paid most of the house bills, except for rent, but it wasn't her home. She also had to follow Daddy's house rules. "What I say goes," he told her.

"Aren't there any police here?" I asked Mamma. She didn't want to have Daddy arrested. When we had gone to the hospital the following day, she lied to the doctors about her broken nose. She told everyone, she had fallen and hit her nose. They knew she wasn't telling the truth. She told us not to say anything, but I wished I had. Jessy was so upset. He wanted to kill Daddy. Mamma told him she didn't want to lose her firstborn son.

"Don't you ever repeat these words," she said to him. Jessy wanted us to leave. Mamma told him we had nowhere to go. We had aunts and uncles, who didn't live too far; why couldn't we go to them, Jessy asked. Things were different in America, Mamma told him. Her brothers and sisters had their own family to worry about.

"Aren't we also family?" Jessy reasserted.

"Here, things are different," Mamma told him again. She looked miserable, repeating the disheartening words over and over again. I wanted to drive my hands through Jessy's teeth to get him to shut his mouth. Though I knew why he was asking. Back home, brothers and sisters relied on one another. Uncles and aunts were like fathers and mothers. Cousins were brothers and sisters. Aunt Clarissa was like Mamma. When her friends came to visit, they could never tell us apart from her own children. Family was different in America.

When we started school, I hated going to class. I still worried a whole lot about Mamma. I was where I wanted to be—home with her. And yet, I was just as miserable as I had been back home. Jessy, as well, I supposed. He started doing drugs. It made him feel *good* he said. But then, he joined a gang. It wasn't because he was a bad kid. He was just scared. He needed protection. Not from Daddy, but from some of the hooligans in the neighborhood. He used to get bullied, walking home from school. Being the new kid on the block, speaking broken English, one had to make friends *real* quick. A year later, Jessy graduated and went away to college. He had escaped Mamma's worst fear. She prayed every day for him not to die young of gang violence. Josie also started hanging out with some bad people. I didn't blame her. They were the only ones in the neighborhood who would talk to us. Nevertheless, Josie came home from school crying one afternoon. She went straight in the shower. This ruffian looking kid walked in with her. He had on gold tooth caps from top to bottom and smelled like wildflower. It was the first time I was meeting her boyfriend. Nothing was coming out of his mouth, except "I'm going to kill this nigga." He looked like the type of guy if I ever got into trouble with, Mamma said, to turn the other cheek and run away. Josie was taking so long in the bathroom; I asked him what happened.

"Somebody ran up on her," he said.

"Who robbed my sister?" I shouted. I was so angry; I began to yell at him for allowing Josie to get mugged. "You fool, she was raped," he said with a shocking gaze. As he perhaps realized he shouldn't have said anything.

"Sis! Sis! Are you all right?" I started to bawl, running after Josie to let me in. She refused to open the door. She made me promise not to tell before finally letting me in.

"I will kill myself if you tell Mamma and Daddy," she said.

Although her boyfriend swore, he was going to have bullets rain on whomever did it, they didn't even know who it was. They had left school early to go to a "hookie" party at a friend's house. Josie had gone into a room upstairs in the house to get a pack of cigarettes from her schoolbag. Someone followed her and threw her down on the bed. It was so dark; she couldn't even make out who it was. Josie's mouth was still covered with blood coming out of the bathroom.

"I begged him to stop," she said, crying in the arms of her boyfriend. The monster who had assaulted Josie kept punching her in the face.

"It's all your fault; why didn't you call the cops?" I asked her boyfriend. It wasn't the way he and his friends handled these matters, he said. I began to despise him ever since that day.

Josie was only sixteen when her innocence was brutally taken from her. "I would hate for something bad to happen to my only girl in this crazy building," Mamma used to say. A horrible thing did happen. I couldn't tell her. It felt as if my lungs were about to fall off, hiding the truth from Mamma. She would die if I were to tell her the awful thing that had happened to Josie. And if Daddy ever found out, Josie, as well, would be going to the grave. She nearly did. I don't know how Daddy found out, but he did. Word must've gotten out at school that Josie got raped. Daddy said he heard about the incident from other parents and quickly realized they were talking about Josie. However, Josie didn't believe him. She thought I was the one who told Daddy. She lied to everyone. Even the police, denying anything ever happened. I knew it was because she didn't want Daddy to think she was at fault. "What did you expect? She's a girl," Daddy said to Mrs. Almenor. She was the social worker who first spoke with Josie. Both of us got a beat down from Daddy. Josie got the worst of it. Daddy slapped her so hard, she nearly fell unconscious. He stooped above her, ramming her face into the ground. Her head pinned to the floor like a balloon.

"You're a bitch; no daughter of mine will be a bitch," Daddy screamed at her. Josie was crying her lungs out, begging for someone to come to her rescue.

"Please, Violin, Mommy, help me," she panted. The cryptic drumbeat and air coming out of her aroused a thirst for blood in me.

When Mamma tried to pull Daddy away, "I better not find out you knew about this," he told her. He wiggled his fingers as if talking to a child. Mamma did not utter a word. She knew better. She simply picked up Josie from the floor and put her to bed. I felt so much anguish for Josie. Her soul had been completely shattered. I loved Josie, but that night was the end of me and her. Mamma kept telling her I was not the one who told Daddy. She told Mamma to stop covering for me. Every single one of Daddy's blows, she said, felt like the coldblooded rapist entering her.

"You're nothing but a big mouth, piece of scum for a brother. I wish Jessy was here," she said. Though she didn't always say it, Josie's loathing of a little brother she once called her hero lingered deeply in her heart.

While away in college, Jessy married this Spanish girl. He didn't want to tell Mamma. His wife was soon about to have a baby. He was about to have his own family and would never return home. He hated Daddy. They spent months not talking to each other. Jessy didn't even greet Daddy farewell when he was leaving. Josie also left to be with her crazy boyfriend; a little over a year after Daddy almost ended her life. It was the last time Daddy put his hands on her. Josie, nonetheless, never forgave him. She couldn't wait to turn eighteen. Back home, it didn't matter. She still would have been considered a child. But in America, she was free to do as she wanted. Back home, Daddy still would have been able to beat her down. And he wouldn't have gone to jail. "You see, Violin," Mamma said, "One place grants you enough freedom to go kill yourself, while the other ruffles its beams so it can kill you with it." Josie didn't finish school. It burned Mamma's heart. Rumor had it that her boyfriend was selling drugs. That wasn't the worst thing, according to Mamma. The few times Josie came to visit, Mamma noticed the bruises on her body. "A rainbow always shines bright even over dark clouds," she'd told Mamma, claiming she was in love. When Mamma pressed Josie to leave her boyfriend, "You're the last person to talk," Josie jeered at her. It tore Mamma apart. Josie stopped visiting after that day. It was just the three of us in the house. Daddy was thrilled with both Jessy and Josie gone. "Ungrateful kids," he called them. If I didn't have to look after Mamma, I also would have left.

I didn't have any friends. "Hey Frenchie," the other kids in the neighborhood would call out to me. "Why are you always walking alone?" they asked. I kind of wanted it that way. Mamma, as well, didn't have many friends. They couldn't be trusted, she said. They will always turn on you. The one friend she had, Daddy chased her away. Ms. Giselle was a nice lady. She and Mamma would sometimes stay home when Mamma wasn't working and watched soap operas all day. "Watch, so you can learn English better," Ms. Giselle used to say to me. I would pretend to be sick and stay home. It was the only time I saw Mamma happy, aside from being with her children. Daddy must have realized what was going on. He came home early one day and kicked Ms. Giselle out of the house. He literally kicked her, Mamma told me. Ms. Giselle didn't fuss too much over the matter. She knew Mamma wouldn't have wanted her to report it to the police. Then again, perhaps she was afraid of immigration. Ms. Giselle didn't have her papers. She was in the U.S. illegally. Daddy didn't want her around. He thought she was pushing Mamma to leave him. A few times, I did hear Ms. Giselle nagging

Mamma about Daddy. "*Move gason*," she called him. I understood why she called him a terrible man—because he was. But he was still my Daddy. Ms. Giselle did give Mamma some great ideas. "This is America; you're a smart woman, with a green card; so go to school," she told her. It was what Daddy feared the most. He didn't want Mamma going to school. In America, once a woman made more money or had a better job than her husband, the man was no longer considered a real man according to Daddy. He told Mamma, Ms. Giselle was too friendly with some of the men in the neighborhood. "She's a bad influence on you," he'd told her.

I couldn't understand why Daddy hated Ms. Giselle so much. It probably had something to do with the credit cards receipts she had helped Mamma find in his closet. Although Mamma never said anything to him, Daddy most likely sensed something was wrong. After Mamma stopped wearing her wedding ring, he took all the papers that were in his closet and threw them out in the trash. Ms. Giselle thought Daddy was having an affair. He had been buying ladies shoes, jewelries, and had even purchased living room furniture.

"I don't know why they called him Dieudonne," Ms. Giselle told Mamma. Daddy's name meant "God given."

Yet, "he's nothing but Lucifer himself," Ms. Giselle joked. She said it with a snicker, but Mamma looked embarrassed. She stared at Ms. Giselle with a forged smile, trying to hide her sadness.

"Everybody's devil looks different," Mamma told her, after Ms. Giselle said it again.

"But his, you can taste; you can smell; and now you can see it with your own eyes," she told Mamma.

I'm sure it didn't take Ms. Giselle for Mamma to find out that Daddy had been with another woman. I didn't know what hurt most; the shame in knowing Daddy was sleeping on another woman's bed, or the harsh beatings she had to endure.

"My devil may have wicked hands, but he sometimes has an angel's heart," Mamma replied to Ms. Giselle.

"If he has a heart inside that evil body of his," Ms. Giselle replied angrily, "he's been doing a whole lot of loving, and not just with you."

It must have been true what Aunt Clarissa said. The devil can hear you even if you talk behind his back. Daddy had to have known Ms. Giselle spoke badly of him. "This woman must not ever come back to this house," he told Mamma. "What the hell is wrong with him? I can't take it anymore," Mamma snapped. But then, she went silent. She never confronted Daddy. She never said a word about him cheating on her. She was afraid of what would happen if she did. She had already suffered too much humiliation in front of her children. When they were back home, Daddy used to go out and leave her in the house all alone, she said. Sometimes, he wouldn't come back until it was daylight again. When Mamma complained, the beatings would get worse. "Trust me, baby boy," Mamma said crying, "With this man, I know when to keep my mouth shut." Daddy often grumbled about not making enough money. What he earned was barely enough to pay the rent. Then why was he paying for another woman's stuff, I asked Mamma.

"The rain has fallen," Mamma sang to herself. "Too much of it has fallen and covered my feet. I better run," she said, "lest it will take me away. I'm drowning."

All Mamma did was go to work, come home, and do it all over again. On the weekends, she would sit in the kitchen by herself and read the Bible. She had no one but me. I felt sorry for her. I started helping around the house. It was the least I could do to show her I loved her. At twelve years old, I was roaming the mean streets of New York City, alone. Flatbush Avenue, in

Brooklyn, was as ferocious as can be. The building we lived in was adjacent to a housing project known as "Vietnam." No matter how ungracious the clamor of a foreign city, I didn't care. It was my adopted home, and Mamma needed my help. She worried a lot about me. I told her, God would protect me. "That's if he really exists," I said. She didn't like that kind of talk.

"Tell the Lord you're sorry, now!'" she said.

I promised her I would, but only if God would answer one thing. "Why does he let Daddy beat you?" I asked. "Why you?"

She put her face down, the floor covered with her tears.

On the weekends, I would wake up early and walk to the laundromat to wash our clothes. I also helped Mamma with buying food for the house. She would fill up the cart with empty cans and bottles for me to recycle when I get to the grocery store. She didn't want me to do it, but I begged her. It felt awesome, helping Mamma: more like relief. She was suffering in silence, with no one to help her.

"Violin, you're my little angel," she would often say. Then Mamma would cry so loudly. "Look at me. Look at me, my son," she lowered her head, gazing into my eyes. The lore of life about to surface from her heart. "I'm tortured, you sacrifice; I'm the one who needs to take care of you," she sulked. I told her the day I would stop helping would be the day I die.

Once, the school called. I didn't return to class, they told Mamma. She left work, came home in the middle of the day, and found me home. I had never had the urge to cut until I saw the other students do it. They would go out a side door, which had a broken lock. I wanted to come home to cook for Mamma. She looked so tired the night before. She came home late and still had to cook. When the doorbell rang, my heart began to race. I didn't answer. Then, the sound of fidgeting keys could be heard outside the door. My heart jerked, thinking it was Daddy coming in. It was Mamma. She walked in with a sad face. She was about to say something but glanced at the stove and noticed dinner had already been prepared. I waited patiently for my punishment. Mamma never wanted me to cook. After school, it's homework time, she said. Mamma glanced at the stove again and gave me a blank stare. She babbled something to herself and drew in a long breath. I knew she was angry. I had rather for her to deal with me than have Daddy find out. *"Wait, what is she doing? Mamma?"* She never said a word. She walked past me and went straight to bed. Ever since that day, I would come home, cook, and then do my homework.

She never asked about that day. It was the last time I cut class.

Life in our building was obscured and full of secrets. In fact, it was like living inside a tower of ruins, or a vastly distressed Babylonian nest. Not just with us, but with all the pretenders. That's what we were, as well as so many others. "How are you doing this blessed day?" Our neighbors would cajole one another. It sounded like taunting. "Great, everything is great," they would all answer, including Mamma, even on her worst days. We all pretended to be happy inside our little nests. I would watch some of the women and their husbands. The women were always smiling with a sparkle in their eyes, telling the world how wonderful life is. But the men, most of them wouldn't utter a word. Some had the face of quiet assassins. Mr. Israel, the young teacher who lived upstairs, I thought was different. He didn't look like the men with pitiless faces. He always had a smile on his face, coming down the stairs. "Stay in school, champ and make that lady proud," he would say to me, whenever he saw me and Mamma coming out of our apartment. I wanted so much to be like him. His wife, Ms. Brookline, was even more endearing. She was a beautiful girl. Ms. Brookline was also a teacher. I used to tell her how I wished she taught at my school. "This little boy has a crush on me," she would say to her husband. It wasn't a crush, or maybe it was. I didn't know what a crush was supposed to feel like.

"I like your name, Miss Brookline," I would say to her. It sounded so much like Mamma's name.

"You have good taste in women," Mr. Israel told me. He said it must've come from Daddy. "Your father also married a beautiful woman," he winked, looking amused.

Come to find out, Ms. Brookline had a lot more in common with Mamma. Her husband was no saint. He was also a woman beater. One night, before going to bed, I heard a loud stomp above my head. It was followed by violent thuds. Though somewhat muffled by the ceiling, the hair-raising blows sounded as if they were coming from inside our apartment. There then was an earth-shattering, banging on our door. It was so loud; it woke up Mamma and Daddy from sleep. They thought there was a riot outside in the hall. "Don't you go near that door now," Daddy barked at me. He must have heard my hasty feet bolting out of my room to see who it was. I didn't care if I took a beating. The woeful roar of a terrified woman was familiar to me. I had a hunch it was Ms. Brookline, crying for help. As soon as I opened the door, she rushed in. "Oh my God! Miss Brookline," I hollered in shock. Her hands shaky, her eyes gawking at me, and her body drenched in blood., she looked as though her tomb was not too far removed from her next breath. It scared the hell out of me.

"Go back upstairs," Daddy told her, "You're going to get us in trouble."

I didn't want her to leave.

"She needs help, call the police," I yelled out.

Ms. Brookline stopped me.

"You stupid little boy, look what you've done now," Daddy growled at me when Ms. Brookline's husband came down.

"Mr. Israel, I'm so sorry," Daddy said to him.

I couldn't believe he was apologizing to a monster.

"It's okay, don't worry about it," Mr. Israel told Daddy. He then kissed Ms. Brookline on the lips.

"Sweetheart, let's go back upstairs," Mr. Israel said to her. I was so disgusted; I almost threw up.

"You know Pappy loves you," Mr. Israel said to his wife.

I couldn't stomach it anymore.

"You're nothing but a piece of crap," I said to him, blood curling through my veins.

"Boy! Where did you learn to speak like that?" Daddy shouted.

"I'm sorry again, Mr. Israel," he said, "This is what America has done to my children."

I felt like telling him it wasn't America. I was too scared. Although shocked the words had come out of my mouth, I had learned them from Daddy. It was what he always told Mamma.

That night was one of the few times I had ever been upset at Mamma. She never came out of her room to help Ms. Brookline or to check up on me. What got me even more boiling mad, was what Ms. Brookline did after her creepy husband nearly beat her to death. She kissed him back. "I love you, too, honey," she said to him on their way back to their apartment. She was just like Mamma. She once told Daddy the same thing, right after he had savagely beaten her and called her a "piece of crap." I was so angry when Mamma did that. I asked her to choose between me and Daddy. He and I almost came to a brawl that day, until I saw Mamma burst into tears. "How can you ask your mother such a thing?" he said. "Either he goes, or I go," I told Mamma. "Wipe your mouth on the floor and say sorry to your father," she said. Daddy was the one who ended up apologizing. "I love your mother, but I can't help it," he said. It stunned me this time, hearing

Daddy say he was sorry. There was something about the way he said it that made me believe it came from his heart.

CHAPTER TWO

It felt as if I was being haunted by the same strange feeling again. The one I had back home when I thought Mamma was in trouble. I was eight then. At thirteen, it had come back to torment me. A frightening chill had been moving through my whole body. My heart pounded so briskly inside my chest; I wanted to run home. I was cringing in fear while at school. By the time I got home, panic had settled inside my belly. Mamma used to tell me to trust my instinct. Once again, the awkward feeling in my gut didn't lie. I could hear her and Daddy arguing even before I had opened the door. My hands were shaky. I fumbled my keys nervously, trying to open the door. It wasn't happening fast enough. There was a nauseating thumping coming from inside the apartment. It sounded like a basketball hitting the wall or someone pounding on a mattress. But it wasn't. Daddy was beating Mamma once again. When I finally opened the door, there were broken glasses everywhere. Daddy threw his foot in the air, hitting Mamma in the face with his long, pointed shoe. I ran and stood in between them. "Stop, please stop," I pleaded with Mamma not to answer him. Daddy didn't like when she talked back. Mamma wouldn't listen to me. I then knelt before her, as if praying to a Saint.

"Mommy, please stop," I begged again.

She started crying. The tears flowing down her cheeks and dropping inside my lips. "My sweet, baby," she cried, with more tears coming out.

They sprinkled my lips like soft rain. It was her heart crying. It was shedding tears of love.

"Don't kneel in front of me, sweetie," Mamma wept.

I told her if she didn't ignore Daddy, my knees would stay planted on the ground.

"Jesus! That's it, no more my child," she said.

I got up and hugged her. It put a smile on her face.

Daddy didn't hit me this time; even though I pulled Mamma away. It may have been because of what I said to him the last time he hit me. I had so much anger within me. I told him if he did it again, one of us would not see another day. I didn't really mean it, but that's how I felt. It might have scared him. Nevertheless, I didn't know what made him so angry with Mamma. He looked like a man possessed. His face was full of hate. Veins were popping out of his forehead as if they were about to explode. He and Mamma weren't even supposed to be home. They worked at the same job; I figured they must have been let out early. Daddy was very jealous. And if he was drunk, his jealous rage would turn him into an even more irrational beast. I saw the bottle of rum on the living room floor. I knew he had been drinking. His breath, however, didn't smell like alcohol. It smelled like vinegar. Perhaps it was all in my mind. Everything smelled and tasted sour. As things were calming down, it would soon be over, I thought. They would make up and kiss all over again. Mamma would hide her tears and love him again. That's the way it had always been. But it was far from over. My hell had just begun.

After she had taken a nap, Mamma said she was going to the pharmacy to get an aspirin. She told me to finish my homework when I offered to get it for her. Besides, she said she needed a breath of fresh air. As soon as she went out the door, Daddy followed her. A few seconds later, "Violine! Violine!" I heard Daddy screaming at the top of his lungs. I ran outside as fast as I could to see why he was yelling so loudly. Daddy was standing in the hallway outside of our apartment with both hands covering his head. His eyes gaping with terror, as if staring at a ghost.

"Where is Mamma?" I asked.

He wouldn't answer. When I looked down the steps, Mamma was lying on the floor.

"Oh my God! Mamma! Mamma! Call an ambulance," I yelled out to Daddy.

I ran down to see how badly Mamma was hurt. Daddy stood motionless.

"I'm so sorry, Violine," he continued to shout.

He had a look of aggravation, shock, and fear balled up into one on his face.

"Mamma, please wake up; don't do this to me; please wake up."

It looked a lot like a bad dream. The ambulance came after I had called them, but it was too late. Mamma died on the way to the hospital. It was the worst day of my life. Tears wanted to come out, but guilt kept them in. I wanted to scream, even louder than I had been shouting inside. I couldn't; what if Mamma's spirit was watching. What would she think of me? When the police asked Daddy what happened, he told them a funny story. However, I wasn't laughing. Daddy told them Mamma accidentally stumbled down the steps on her way to the store. He told the detective, he and I were inside the house talking, and quickly ran out when we heard a loud thump outside the door.

"Is that what happened?" Detective McKenna asked.

"Yes, yes sir," I said to him.

The room—cold—my body shivering with fear, they asked the same questions a million times.

"Did they have a fight?' someone else asked.

He was a much friendlier detective, a lot more compassionate than the others.

"No," I answered, all the while thinking about how Daddy quickly cleaned up his mess before the police and ambulance showed up.

"Your brother says your dad beats up on your mom all the time," Detective McKenna said, over and over again.

I was getting tired of him asking the same questions.

"Daddy didn't do anything wrong," I told him, each time he'd asked.

By this time, I was beyond exhausted. My eyes felt heavy. I just wanted to go home. I wanted to go to sleep and never wake up. They had all four of us at the police station., including Daddy. Jessy was the only one talking. Undoubtedly, it was solely because he hated Daddy. Still, he also liked to beat on his wife and kids. My niece and nephew were toddlers; too young for the slap across the face whippings Jessy called punishment. He was afraid to say too much. His wife was so quiet at the station. They couldn't wait to go back home. Josie was too scared to talk. Her crazy boyfriend sold drugs and likewise, beat up on her. Daddy had to defend himself at all costs. He didn't want to go to jail.

Before the police and ambulance got to the house, Daddy made me promise not to say anything. He said he would handle it. But when he did, he didn't tell the truth. "If they think I did anything, they will lock me up," he said. He then told me I would have to live with people I didn't know. They would place me in foster care. I had no one to go to. "You know your mom's family don't give a damn about you," he made certain to remind me. It was the only thing that came out of his mouth that wasn't a lie. If they didn't care about Mamma when she was getting beat up, they surely didn't care if I was dead or alive. They never once came around to see how we were doing. Daddy didn't have any family in America. I could have gone to live with either Jessy or Josie, but Daddy was very smart. He knew I hated Jessy.   Staying with Josie and her boyfriend would have been like living in a drug factory. Even so, Daddy knew it wasn't my only reason for not giving him up. I loved him; not more than Mamma, but it was very close. He used to tell me, "Son, watch when you grow up, you're going to be just like me." I was his favorite child, he told me. I once told Mamma, I thought Daddy hated me just as much as he hated her because we didn't look like him. She said it was foolish of me to think that way. Daddy loved us just as he loved his pale-skinned children. "Trust me, he loves us just as much," Mamma avowed with a stone face. "Even roses have thorns," she said. Though I still loved Daddy, part of me began to despise him even more.

CHAPTER THREE

My first day of high school was in the fall of 1986. It was about a year after Mamma died. Perhaps Daddy felt guilty about what had happened to Mamma. He bought me a lot of fresh clothes and had even become more lenient with me. I had enough gear to last me the whole year. Taking the bus on my way to school my first day, a new life was about to begin. I carried my Walkman like a music box on my hip. My headphones blasting, listening to hip hop music. My world was full of life once again. I was only fourteen, but it felt as though I was king. I had a fresh cut fade, brand new outfits, and my steps had a bounce to them. It was mostly because of what was playing in my ears. Mamma used to tell me that type of music could make you lose your soul. Yet, it gave me one. If only she could see me now, I thought. She would have been proud. She would have said, "Sweetie, I'm your number one fan." And I would have answered, "You know it, Mamma; I'm also your number one fan." I started feeling sad again. The pain buried inside began to burn my chest. The melody lifted me up. It gave me hope. It was like feeling the warmth of a cool autumn wind, like rootless love chasing after the heart. It wasn't gangster music like Daddy said. It took me to a new place. I was breathing again.

I walked into my first period orientation class that day with my head held high, just like Mamma taught me. I was no longer the "Frenchie" teen the neighborhood kids used to call me. I sat in the back of the room waiting for class to start; never in my wildest dreams thought my entire world was about to change. The classroom lit up. My belly started to ache. I heard the crowing of birds in my head. The most beautiful girl I had ever seen walked in and sat next to me. "Oh Jeez," I said out loud. Everyone in the class began to laugh. The girl was so pretty; she had my heart pounding as though it were rocking to a dope beat.

"Hello to you too," she said, arcing her soulful lips with a smile.

"Oh. My. God," I let out, not knowing what else to say.

Her perfume ran through my senses like a bolt of lightning. She repeatedly gazed at me, each time provoking a covetous rush. I was afraid to look back. I wasn't shy, talking to girls. She was so gorgeous, every time I would stare at her, my heart would get feathery. When class ended, she and I stayed back. As the Lord would have it, like Mamma used to say; we both happened to have the same class in the same room the following period.

"Violin, right?" she asked with a sweet voice.

"That's my name," I told her: my heart hammering inside my chest.

"Why won't you look at me?" she asked.

I had been, though she didn't know it. She had asked the teacher for a restroom pass. As I watched her walking out of the room, time stood still. She was moving on air. Her hips wiggled, as though tapping to a slow jam. Her lips looked so soft and glittery. She must have had diamonds sprinkled on them. She was beyond stunning. Nadine was the girl of my dreams.

Nadine and I became good friends. As ninth graders, we had some of the same classes. So, we hung out a lot. After school, she and I would sometimes go to the park and shoot hoops. I didn't know anything about basketball. I had been too busy helping Mamma.

I acted as though I did. And Nadine pretended as though she didn't realize that I couldn't play. A girl, the girl of my dreams, taught me how to play. She made me feel like a man. I wanted the little boy in me to go away. Nadine liked to call me sweetie. It sounded so much different than the way Mamma used to say it.

"Why do they call you Violin?" she asked.

I told her I was named after Mamma.

"What is that?"

She couldn't understand why I called my mother, Mamma. I told her that's how most kids referred to their mothers back home.

"it's actually Manman, but I prefer to call my mother, Mamma."

"I see," she laughed.

She then wanted to know where home was; so, I told her.

"Ah, no wonder you have this weird accent," she said.

Though Nadine was born in Brooklyn, her parents were also from the islands. The girl of my dreams; the prettiest girl I had ever known wanted to know everything about me. It felt so heartwarming. It was dreamlike, just like her touch. Once, she must have noticed my lips were perhaps a bit flaky, beaten by the cold air while waiting for the bus. She took some good smelling cream out of her schoolbag and rubbed it over my lips. It smelled just like her. It was a sweet blend of strawberry and coconut oil. As she was running her fingers over my mouth, my heart started jumping. So many parts of me were moving, which I was not able to control. I felt a little embarrassed. But it was not her fault; Nadine did not notice. There was no way for her to know what she was doing to me.

Nadine told me I was the strangest kid she had ever met. When she heard me listening to a classical tune one day, she looked amazed. "Why do you listen to that?" she asked. Though hip hop gave me soul, classical music had kept me alive. Growing up back home, the stringing harp of its melody comforted me, whenever I thought about Mamma. It was the breath of life of my fantasy world. It gave me relief when madness threatened to take me young. It gave me strength when I would hear the depressing blows crushing Mamma. While starring in a play in drama class as *Augustin*, a 16th century French soldier, the symphonies came back in my head. As we were nearing the end of a climactic scene, Augustin ran to save his lover, who had accidentally fallen on Augustin's sword. Sobbing with deep-seated grief, he held her in his arms.

"Wake up, wake up," he wailed, *"and tell me you love me."*

The room suddenly turned dark. *"Wake up, wake up, Mamma,"* I wept, *"and tell me you love me."* She had fallen asleep in my arms. There was then, these loud jeers all over the room. Nadine hurried to my rescue and rested my head on her chest. Everything was at a standstill, as everyone continued to laugh. The girl of my dreams had covered my shameful mien.

"State your name for me," Mr. Pierre-Louis asked.

"My name is Violin Labonne," I answered.

"What's your father's name?" he then asked, after a curious pause.

"His name is Dieudonne Labonne," I said to him.

"What!" Mr. Pierre-Louis almost fell off his chair.

"THE SON OF THE FAMOUS DIEUDONNE LABONNE! I cannot believe it."

He apparently knew Daddy back home. Daddy was once a schoolteacher. Yet, I never thought of him as being famous.

"What is your father doing now?" Mr. Pierre-Louis asked.

I told him Daddy worked at a sculpting factory.

"Oh, that's too bad," he said, "Your father was an excellent schoolteacher."

Mr. Pierre-Louis told me he knew both Jessy and Josie. He lost contact with Daddy after an argument over Mamma.

"How is that pretty lady doing?" he asked.

I didn't want to tell him.

"She's dead now," I finally let off, feeling my chest tense up.

"So sad to hear, was she ill?" he asked.

I stared at him for a long time without a word. He knew. Mr. Pierre-Louis may not have figured out all the details; he, nonetheless, sensed something horrible had happened. He didn't force me to answer.

"May her soul rests in peace," he said. Then, his face got a lot more serious than it had been. He swallowed whatever was in his throat and exhaled a long breath over his thick mustache. My English literature teacher wanted him to talk to me. The poems I had been writing in class were somewhat disturbing, the teacher told him. Mr. Pierre-Louis taught French literature. When I told him, my prose may have been misunderstood because of where I was from—being a Haitian immigrant—his answer was, "When you sell your soul to the devil, expect to return that money back." I never took literature again. Daddy never found out about Mr. Pierre-Louis. I didn't want to tell him. After our conversation, whenever Mr. Pierre-Louis would see me in the school hallway, he would turn his head, pretending not to see me. It must have been his way of telling me he did not want to get involved.

I was growing into my own man after Mamma died. Perhaps Nadine had something to do with it. Daddy also started to show me more respect. I had often wondered, if it was because he was afraid that I would tell everyone the truth. He and I were becoming friends. We didn't talk about Mamma a whole lot. The big secret was eating at us both. We acted as though nothing was wrong. It was tearing Daddy apart from inside out. The doctor told him he was diabetic, and his blood pressure was high. It's a good thing it happened. He then stopped drinking. Daddy started to look old. He was in his early forties, but he looked as if he was sixty. His head was full of grey hair. As he and I were watching television one night, Daddy started to cry. Something must have been terribly wrong. I had never seen Daddy cry. He didn't even shed a tear the day Mamma died. Not even the day she was buried. His face never looked gentle. Even when he smiled, one could spot his fiery temper.

"Son," he said, "I have something to tell you."

I started to worry; thinking he was going to tell me he was dying. Daddy knelt in front of me, just as I had done the day Mamma died.

"Son," he once again called out to me, with more tears pouring out.

"My love did it," he said.

"Did what Daddy? What are you talking about?" I asked.

He'd killed Mamma, he told me. Daddy finally admitted it. He wasn't confessing a secret. I knew what he had done. He didn't mean to do it, he said.

"I killed her in a fit of rage," Daddy cried out. "Please forgive me; please forgive me, my son," he pleaded.

Daddy thought Mamma had been cheating on him with somebody at work. That day, something came over him as he followed Mamma out in the hallway. He shoved her. He pushed Mamma down the stairs. A jealous rage had taken over his heart. Resentment had driven him over the edge. Daddy then hugged me. His deafening, desolate cry, echoed inside of me. His head rested on my lap, while he firmly wrapped his hands around my waist. The front of my shirt drenched with his tears.

I was seventeen years old, about to graduate from high school when Daddy confessed. Although he didn't have to; it somewhat freed me, hearing it out of his lips. It had only been a secret because he and I didn't talk about it. Once he told me, the heavy burden of guilt had been lifted off my chest. For a long time, it felt as if my hands were in it. I had Mamma's blood splattered all over me like a condemned soul. The next day, I told Nadine about it. I trusted her enough not to get Daddy arrested. "What are you going to do?" she asked. "Nothing, there's nothing to be done but hope and pray no one finds out," I told her. I wasn't going to tell on Daddy. He was the only family I had. Josie and I were once very close, but she put her man above me. Jessy did the same with his wife and kids. I had no one but Daddy, and Nadine, of course, but she was only my friend. Though Nadine may not have known; deep within me, I worshipped her. I wanted something more, like what Jessy and Josie had. Neither of them had a perfect life, but they both had somebody to love.

Spring has a way of bringing out the hidden beauty in everything. In the spring of 1990, the best year of my life was about to reach its apex. Throughout my years in high school, I never had a girlfriend. I loved Nadine, but I never told her. Besides, she started going out with this husky looking guy on the football team. Since it was our senior year, and with graduation looming, it was time to get ready for prom night. Nadine had a friend she wanted me to go to the prom with. It was not the most appealing idea. The girl wasn't ugly at all. She was as pretty as Nadine, if not more. My heart, however, belonged to Nadine. When Tiffany, Nadine's friend, called to ask me out to the prom, I told her I would go with her; yet made her promise to do one thing.

"Tell Nadine I love her," I finally let out. Fully aware her sole reason for asking me out to the prom was as a favor to Nadine. Tiffany laughed when I confessed my love. Then, she uttered what a lonely young man had been longing to hear.

"She feels the same way," Tiffany muttered, extending her laugh.

"Oh Jeez!" I screeched out; my cheeks almost exploding with the loud shout.

"You say that often, Nadine says," Tiffany mocked. "Wow, sounds like you really have it bad for her."

May 1990, Café Olivier Amour, Brooklyn, New York.

Tiffany and I arrived at a crowded ballroom, already filled with school administrators and students. All eyes were on us. Not so much because of me. Tiffany looked gorgeous in her white satin gown. We both wore white; looking as if we were about to get married. Nadine and I spoke a few times before the prom. Neither of us said anything about what I had told Tiffany to tell her. On prom night, however, she showed up at the café, alone. The joke was on me, apparently. The minute she walked in, "there goes your girl," Tiffany blurted out. My prom date was about to walk out on me. This guy, out of nowhere, shoved his way past me, snatching Tiffany away.

"Sorry, Tiffany is my date," he said.

I began to sweat with a cold heave inside of me. It felt as if I had been abandoned at the altar. It was going to be the most embarrassing night of my life or the best night ever. Then, the girl of my dreams walked up to me and extended her hands.

"Let's dance," she said. My heart jolted. I felt a powerful surge within me, like the stream of the ocean waves, like waterfalls. As I got closer, Nadine leaned over, pressing her lips against my cheek.

"Oh Jeez!" she whispered, softly.

"Praise God," I said out loud.

We both started to laugh. Mamma wasn't lying; prayer is a good thing. I had prayed to have a moment like this. One, I never thought would come true. Nadine moved closer. Her chest rising like a towering wave against my body. My ribs shivered with each breath. Her caramel mustard skin, delicately stroking my face; I wanted to kiss her every time we touched. There was this warm breeze wafting through my chest.

"So, the joke was on me?" I asked. As Nadine and I talked in the backroom lounge. Ben, her boyfriend, was now an ex, she said with a sweet grin. She looked more beautiful than ever in her body-hugging, black lace dress. Our first day of high school, she looked like a cute girl. Prom night, I was staring at a stunning young woman.

"Come here," she said.

I wasn't quite sure what she wanted me to come to. We were in a dark room, with school officials and other students just a few doors away.

"Come here, Violin," her voice frisky, yet commending.

This time, the way she squealed out my name, I knew she was serious.

"What if we get caught?" the words fluttered out of my lips. *Is it only going to be a kiss?* I had never been with a girl before. After approaching her, Nadine pressed her lips against mine. She then sat on my lap. Her fragrance overpowered me to the tune of "One Last Time." It was the song playing in the background. When she moved, I moved. When she cried, I cried.

"I love you, Violin," Nadine loosened her grip with fainting breaths. She wept, clutching my head between her palms, both of our bodies shivering. It was the first time I had ever heard these words since Mamma died. It was my first kiss. My first love. My first waltz, far below the waist of a woman.

CHAPTER FOUR

In the summer of 1990, I graduated from high school with a nearly perfect GPA. I'm not sure how it happened, but I did. Graduation was rather bittersweet. I wished Mamma was there to see me. She would have been proud, seeing her youngest son graduating from high school. I cried a lot that day. Not just because of Mamma. Daddy couldn't make it to the graduation ceremony. He had a lot on his mind, he said. Nadine lifted my spirit. She sat next to me, holding my hands. "You're a man now," she said. Was I? Most times, I felt like a little boy, except when Nadine was around. I was scared, deathly afraid that life was going to devour me. Nadine wanted to go away to college. I told her I wouldn't be able to come along. Who was going to look after Daddy? Neither Jessy, nor Josie cared if he was dead or alive. They showed up and stayed long enough to see me stroll with my cap and gown on stage. But then they both claimed they had to leave. They had stuff at home to take care of, they said. Nadine's family was kind enough not to allow their callous snub to ruin my day. They took me out to dinner and bought me a cake and balloons. They did whatever they could to make the day feel special. It was all Nadine's idea, according to her dad. At the restaurant, Nadine warmed my heart once more. She had her parents sing to me. She remembered it was also my birthday. It had turned into the anniversary of death.

"Are you Nadine's boyfriend?" her father asked.

"No sir, we're only friends," I answered, looking at Nadine with her head down.

"She sure has me doing a whole lot for a so-called friend," he uttered with an air of sarcasm, emptying out his wallet.

The black rum cake tasted sour. "Too much, too much lemon," Nadine's mother complained.

"Come on! Maribel, what good thing in life does not later taste a little bitter," Nadine's father said, laughing.

When I got home, Daddy wasn't around. I figured he must have gone out to get something at the store.

Ever since Mamma died, he didn't go out much. When I went into his room, something strange caught my eyes. There was an open bottle of rum on the dresser. Daddy promised he wasn't going to drink anymore. I couldn't wait for him to get home to chew him out. I looked out the window; a police car made a U-turn and parked in front of the building. Somebody is getting arrested again, I thought to myself. This was an everyday thing where we lived. It was one of the reasons I told Daddy, after graduating, I would get a job so we both could move to a nicer place. Still, I loved most of the people in our neighborhood. Good or bad, they had always been there for us. I was not about the thug life, however. Many of them showed me respect for wanting to be my own man. One thing I found out about living in the hood; a lot of times, the people around are more loyal than the outside world. Even the ones who were selling drugs used to watch over Mamma. It had been close to ten years since we lived in the neighborhood. I got to know them, as they got to know me. Not all the dope dealers were monsters.

I was getting worried. *"Where is Daddy, already?"* I pondered, looking out the window and feeling restless. I jiggled my feet until the sole of my left foot began to hurt. Mamma said it was bad luck to only have one foot hurting. It was a symptom of an evil spirit entering someone's heart. I'm not sure I believed her. Yet it always made me afraid. Now I really had reasons to be. Perhaps Daddy wanted to surprise me. Maybe he was out getting me a birthday gift. Nadine called; she wanted to come over. I told her she didn't have to. If Daddy didn't show up in a couple of hours, I was going to call the police. Nadine had yet to meet Daddy. She hadn't even been to the house. I wasn't comfortable talking to Daddy about these things. He was not that kind of father. After Mamma died, he and I got close, but I still wanted to keep Nadine a secret. "*McKenna?'* Oh shoot, it's Detective McKenna," I shouted out. He was coming out of an unmarked car. He's the one who had interviewed me at the police station the day Mamma died. Whatever was going down had to be awfully serious. I started to think, we may have another dead body in the building. Suddenly, there was a loud knock on the door. Panic was settling in. I ran to the door without even asking who it was, thinking it was Daddy.

"Where the heck were you?" I hollered.

It wasn't Daddy; it was Detective McKenna. He was standing outside of the door with a uniformed officer. Were they coming to arrest me or Daddy? My goodness, it was my graduation day. No wonder the dealers down the block said the cops didn't care about us.

"Son," the detective said, "We need to talk."

Why was he calling me son? It had to be a trap.

"Detective McKenna, if this is about Daddy, I don't know anything," I told him.

"Please, let's grab a seat," he waved to the uniformed officer to wait by the door.

I told him I didn't want to sit. Anything he had to tell me, he should say it and leave.

"This is about your dad," he said, his eyes bloody red.

It had been a little over four years since Detective McKenna and I last spoke. He had always treated me with respect. But there was no way he was going to make me give up Daddy's ghost. It was an accident.

"Your father has turned himself in," Detective McKenna quietly muttered.

"Get out my house! Both of you," I shouted. My head spinning and my body burning with raging fire.

Those dealers weren't lying; these cops were shifty. *How dare he?* I'm thinking. All the while holding my breath that it isn't true. "Daddy would never do that," I said, "You know why? Because he didn't do it."

Detective McKenna stared at me; his eyes gaping with a look of pity. "Do you know where your father is at this moment?" he asked.

I had no idea what to say to him.

"Exactly," he pounced.

I couldn't believe it. What had Daddy done? "He's at the station," Detective McKenna said. My knees started to shake. Perhaps Daddy may have said too much because he got drunk. But when I got to the station, Daddy said he thought about drinking, but then ditched the rum down the toilet.

"Son, I deserve the penalty of my sins," he said.

I fought him, struggling as best as I could with my words for him not to do it. He wouldn't listen to me.

"I love you, son. And happy birthday," Daddy cuddled my fists with his hands. "You're a man now," he sobbed, "so do the right thing."

I refused to let him go. Tears of bitterness flowing out of me, I wept incessantly. "They can't prove it, Daddy; they can't prove it," I cried out. My throat throbbing. I wanted to rip everyone at the station into pieces.

They had a witness. The old lady next door saw what had happened that day. She was afraid to say anything. Mrs. Reid was the one who had allowed Mamma to use her phone the night Daddy kicked us out. When she learned I had told the police, Daddy was in the apartment with me when Mamma fell to her death, she thought I would be in trouble if she said anything. Daddy heard her looking out the peephole. She always did, whenever there were any sorts of melee in the hallway. Daddy knew she wouldn't tell. In spite of her trepidation in wanting to protect me. Where we lived, it was best to mind your own business. Daddy went to see Mrs. Reid before going to the station. She served as witness. Although I had covered up for Daddy, since I was only thirteen at the time, they didn't give me any jail time. The judge was so angry. He sentenced Daddy ten to fifteen years in prison. It was a light sentence, he said, compared to what Daddy could've gotten. The DA wanted him to serve more for getting me involved. There was a good chance Daddy would get out early on parole since he turned himself in. "I have no reason not to have faith in your son's plea for leniency," the judge told him, believing Mamma's death was an accident.

Jessy and Josie shouted with joy when they found out Daddy had been put in jail for killing Mamma. "He's getting what he deserves," they said. They were both hypocrites. Jessy was playing judge to a sin he narrowly escaped. His wife nearly lost her life after one of his violent outbursts. She refused to press charges. A neighbor found her unconscious in Jessy's car, parked in the driveway. She was almost choked to death.

Jessy's wife told the police a stranger did it. I knew it was a lie. When I told Jessy, I would tell the police the truth if he ever did it again, he cut me with a dagger that made my stomach turned. "Tell them, just like you told on Daddy," he said. As for Josie, she was a wreck. She called asking for money, telling me she had lost her job. She was not telling the whole truth. I found out she was in a drug rehab facility. Our once proud family had been torn apart. Though I had become close to Daddy, I started hating him again. It was his fault. It all started because of him. If he didn't do what he did to Mamma, beating on her all the time, and finally killing her, then maybe, Jessy and Josie wouldn't have turned out the way they did. Although Daddy said I was just like him, I wasn't. I was more like Mamma. I had her blood, her heart, and starless genes.

CHAPTER FIVE

After Daddy went to prison, I didn't have many options. It was hard finding a job. Even if I had one, it probably wouldn't be enough to keep up with the rent. I wanted to move out of the house anyway. There were too many bad memories. It was time for a fresh start. I didn't know where I was going. I had to find a place to stay. Faced with few choices, I stayed with Jessy for a while. I told him if he ever beat his wife or kids in front of me, there would be fireworks between us. I started working as a security guard in the city until I could figure out what to do. Nadine, as well, had a lot to think about. She insisted on going away to college. She started feeling sick all the time. She told me she would wait a year, work, then we both could go to this university, Upstate, New York. I wasn't sure what to do with my life anymore. Daddy locked up in Rikers, although I hated him even more, I wanted to stay close in case something were to happen to him. He was already in poor health. I worried he might die soon. My whole world seemed stuck in a box. That's when it happened. My life was about to go through another change.

"You need to come down right away," Nadine's voice soared in panic. She wanted me to come down to Brooklyn, fast. She wouldn't tell me what it was about. Since I didn't have a car, I took the train and a bus. When I got to her house, the whole family was in the living room waiting. I didn't even know her dad was back from his trip to England. It scared the life out of me, seeing him in the living room. His eyes, along with his towering shoulders, appeared to be shadowing me the moment I walked in. I knew Nadine was deathly afraid of her parents. But for her not to even warn me, it had to be something bad. She wasn't even around.

"Where is Nadine?" I asked.

Her mom told me she was in her room.

"Sit down, boy," Nadine's father placed an impaled wooden chair in front of me, a harsh and sneering tone in his voice.

Nadine's mom looked on with a demure spirit. She held on to both of my hands, running her fingers gently over my damp knuckles.

"She pregnant, you know," she calmly uttered with her piercing Caribbean accent.

"What!"

I almost dropped to the floor.

"Mama, are you serious?"

I couldn't believe what came out of her lips.

"Yes, dear. My baby, my sweet little angel is pregnant," she said, the pain in her voice — brash, and the agony on her face — bold.

I noticed Nadine standing behind me. I hadn't seen her in over a month. She didn't look pregnant.

"Sweetie, it's true," she said.

"We God fearing people," Nadine's father yelled out, "We don't believe in abortion."

"Sir," I started to answer, about to tell him that I wanted to marry his daughter.

"Listen very carefully young man," he cut me off. He stood up; his voice rising with every syllable. "My daughter promised me she was going to be a lawyer but look! Look what you've done," he flung his chair across the room. "I told her never to date a Caribbean man," he said, extending his index finger down at me like a shooting dart.

"Mr. Leon, Sir, I'm asking to marry your daughter. I love Nadine; I want to marry her," I said to him.

He seemed lost in his own world.

"You're going to take responsibility for the child," he shouted.

The more he talked, the louder his voice sliced me with insults. Nadine's mom, her older brother, three of her uncles, and her mom's sister, all stood around quietly heeding her father's scathing words.

"Mr. Leon, Mr. Leon," I called out to him.

He either must not have heard me or simply didn't care to listen. I got up and bowed on my knees in front of Nadine. Her Dad finally stopped speaking. Everyone else, likewise, kept their silence. "Nadine, I love you. You're the only girl I've ever loved. Will you marry me?" I vowed for her to become my bride.

Nadine's aunt and her mom had tears in their eyes. I stayed on my knees and looked up. Droplets of Nadine's tears sprinkled down and slid between my lips. I looked at the men in the room; they all had teary eyes.

"Yes, you can have me," Nadine stood over me, running her hands over my face.

More of her tears entered my mouth. As I was getting up, I heard the faint thuds of applauses. They were coming from the room but seemed so far away. Something was happening to me. I felt a fiery throb inside. It was choking me with my own anger. *"Go away, go away,"* I wrestled with my thoughts for the fury to leave me. I kissed Nadine, hoping the suffocating madness would end. Her lips tasted bitter. What in the world was happening to me?

October 1990, Nadine, and I finally got married. She was five months pregnant with twin girls. I was so thrilled they were girls. They wouldn't have any traces of Daddy in them. It was a small ceremony. Only Nadine's family showed up. Josie was still struggling with drugs. Jessy promised to come, but later said he had better things to do. It ended our brotherhood that day. It was the last time we spoke. Nadine and I lived in the basement at her parents' house. It gave us a place to stay until the twins were born. It irked me, living under the same roof with her parents. They poked their noses too much into our affairs. I didn't like it, but I didn't have a choice. The security job paid just above minimum wage. Still, it wasn't enough. Trying to survive on five dollars an hour in New York City was like blending water, hoping for it to turn into cooking oil, as many used to say back home. "Soon baby, I'm going to get us out of here, soon," I told Nadine. The girl of my dreams became everything to me. She was teaching me how to be a man.

The day we left home to be with Mamma was the happiest day of my life. The day Nadine became my wife was a close second. But the day she gave birth to my twin girls, death wanted to ruin my best day. "Come to the hospital, now!" Nadine's mother shouted as soon as I picked up. I was at work; I rushed out of there so fast, hardly anyone noticed I was gone. Nadine was in a lot of pain. When the first of my girls was coming out, Nadine nearly stopped breathing. Her blood pressure plummeting, her eyes turned red, her heart spluttering inside her chest. The doctors ordered us out of the room. Nadine's pressure was dropping like the freefall of a death slide. "Come back, baby. Come back," I yelled out to her, feeling my heart in my throat. She still was not responding. "Nadine, I love you; please don't leave me. Don't do this to me," I screamed out as they were escorting me out. "Don't do it, Lord. Don't do it," I fell out on the floor, feeling a part of me dying.

My best day ever, threatened to also be my worst. Mamma always told me, if you prayed hard enough, it would open God's ears. So, I prayed—loudly and fast. I didn't really know what to say. I had been angry with God for taking Mamma away. Finally, when it felt as if my words weren't enough, I pounded my chest with my right fist.

"Don't let my babies die," Nadine's mother cried out.

"Yes Lord," her father shouted back. He then sat next to me on the floor. "Get a hold of yourself, young man. She's going to be all right," he said.

I was so afraid to lose my wife. A few minutes later, the doctor came to get us. All three of my girls were doing well. Nadine came close to her last breath. I told her it was not yet her time. Holding both of my daughters in my arms, I thought of Mamma. She would have been proud.

I went to visit Daddy to show him pictures of his twin baby girls. It made him even more miserable. "Son," he said, "Love can make you do some weird things." He wished he could take back that day. I tried to console him. Staring into the desolate eyes responsible for my pain and grief, I saw peace, yet a storm out of hell brewing.

"You know what I think," Daddy lowered his voice. "Hell is up here," he said, beating his temple with his fingers.

No matter what I said to make him feel better, guilt still ate at him.

"I loved your mother. Violine was a good woman. She saw things in me I couldn't even feel myself. My sin is ravaging me like a cancer," Daddy said, weeping.

"I might as well be dead, Violin. I might as well be dead," he jerked his head.

I felt pity for him. It was one of the few times I ever did.

"Violin, you're now a father, just like me," he said, wiping his face with his hands. "The day you were born, I only saw you for a couple of hours," he bowed his head and began to cry again. Daddy worked as a dishwasher on a cruise ship. He sailed back to America, because work was the only sure way for him to get Mamma to join him. Daddy told me he wished he could've abandoned the ship that day and not leave his family behind.

"I worked hard, Violin, for my family to make it here in America," Daddy lifted his head, eyeing the ghostlike stall. "Everything is lost in me chasing a dream," Daddy pounded his fists against one another. "It's time for you to go," he said.

After our girls were born, Nadine wanted to go back to school. Since we were still living with her parents, I figured she would take a few classes at the college down the block until we sorted things out. She dropped a bombshell. She wanted to go Upstate to study law, leaving her mom to care for our girls. "Heck no," I told her. Her mother offered to look after the kids. She and I could both go Upstate to finish school. I'm a man I told Nadine. I take care of my own. She said she was leaving with or without my approval. I knew it was because of her father. He wanted so badly for Nadine to be a lawyer. He pushed her to get a scholarship from a school, Upstate. That's when things started to go sour between me and Nadine. "Where does that leave me?" I asked. She chose to listen to her father instead of her husband. "You don't love me," I pleaded with her the night she was leaving. It had nothing to do with love, she said. "I need to do better," Nadine shrugged me off, dismissing the potential risk to our marriage. Leaving her children and husband behind, I told her, was the ultimate abandonment. It didn't matter what her motives were. If she truly loved me, she would stay. She ignored my plea. Nadine left. She took away my love. I hated her. A few weeks later, I moved out of her parents' house.

Why didn't Mamma tell me raising kids would be such a burden? Why didn't Daddy teach me? I was trying my best to take care of my two girls. Yet, it seemed the more I did, the more I had to fend off Nadine's mother's insults. "They need this, they need that," her mother boggled my ears every day. It was never enough. Her list of complaints almost drove me insane. Every week, she expected me to send money. Why couldn't she understand; I wasn't making enough. "Well get a better job," she said. As if it were that easy. So, I bolted, leaving town without telling anyone. I wasn't purposely trying to walk away from my kids. I felt empty, angry at the world and Daddy, but mostly with Nadine. I only knew how to be a man around her.

I was twenty years old, feeling like a ten-year-old little boy. What did a real man look like anyway, Daddy? Jessy? The only real man I had ever known was Uncle Ronald. He was miles away. I had tried to call him a few times. He couldn't even speak. Aunt Clarissa said he had suffered a stroke. I told her; I would visit soon. Not soon enough for my never-ending grief. Uncle Ronald went home to be with Mamma. Life wasn't being fair to me. A boyhood temper was whirling inside of me like a storm. I went home. I spent four days. I couldn't wait to come back. The first night, I heard Mamma crying. The next night, the day of Uncle Ronald's funeral, Mamma died in my sleep. The third night, I died. I saw familiar faces at Uncle Ronald's burial. Many of which, I had not seen since Mamma died. They all tried to pin their guilt on Daddy. Telling me how much they hated him; enough to forsake their own blood. "See you around," they said. "Sure, we'll keep in touch when I get back to the U.S.," I replied. It was what family had become in America. They couldn't even pretend to love me.

"You're beginning to look so much like your dad," Aunt Jasmine said. No wonder she couldn't look at me square in the eyes. Long ago, she would bake cakes, and stuff our moths with lots of candies, when Jessy, Josie, and I would stay at her house during school breaks. I remember her telling me she wanted to adopt me as her son. Aunt Clarissa would get jealous, terrified we wouldn't come back. Things were different now. The day I was leaving, I saw death in Aunt Clarissa's eyes. She, as well, went home to be with Mamma. I didn't stay to watch her get buried. I knew life would end up breaking my will one day. And it did. I descended into hell. I stopped visiting Daddy. Nadine and I no longer talked. We weren't divorced, but I knew once she or her parents found me, it was going to be the end of our marriage. "You have to learn to let go of resentment," I remember Mamma telling me. It would have been better to go Upstate with Nadine, I started thinking. My pride wouldn't allow it. Being away from her, life wasn't as gratifying. I missed my kids. Something inside of me, nonetheless, was pushing me to run.

I made California my home. I stayed with this girl whom Nadine and I went to school with. I told her, Nadine and I were separated. I needed a place to stay. We weren't the best of friends in high school. Simone, however, always looked out for me. She lived on her own and worked at a casino. Not too long after moving in, she got me a gig at the casino. I wasn't performing on stage, but I might as well had been. It was a security job, which I very much despised. I would have to send money for my kids. I worried about Nadine's parents haunting me down for child support. I loved my girls and wanted to take care of them. I just needed to get away for a while.

Simone didn't do much, aside from working, come home and cook, and watch the news every night. She didn't like to go out. I watched her do the same thing, months after months. It was rather unusual for such a pretty girl not to have men flocking to her nest. She didn't even date. Simone wanted to get married, but her own demons appeared to be tearing at her heart. She wouldn't admit it. And yet, I sensed she couldn't figure out whom she wanted to settle with, a man or a woman.

"Is that why you've moved so far?" I asked.

"Whomsoever my heart wants," she replied coldly, nearly smashing her cup of tea on the counter. "What really makes my heart sick," she said, irritably wiping the droplets of tea on the counter with her hands," we live in a world where you can't be yourself."

The solution always seems so plain in vetting someone else's pain. "I love you," I told Simone.

"A lot of people do, until I pour my heart out," she replied.

As she and I sat on the couch, watching television, Simone was all over my mind. I didn't know what it was, but something came over me. I had never been with any other woman but Nadine. I wanted Simone. It had been close to three years since Nadine and I separated. It still felt as though I would be committing a sin. Simone said she had rather wait until she finds true love. I was scared. There was this battle brewing inside of me. My head was telling me to show respect. My body singing a different tune. Simone and I had come close to breaking our vows. We always found the will to turn away. What if she rejects me, my mind wandered? For nearly three years under the same roof, we resisted the urge. It was getting too much to bear.

"Violin, I know what you're thinking," Simone puckered her brow, leering my way.

She must have noticed the lust in my eyes.

"It's different for me too, tonight," she said.

As she spoke, my mind began to race. My whole inside burning hot. Was I about to commit the ultimate sin? "I've only been with one woman," I told Simone. She laughed. She said her only time was with her best friend in high school. Nadine had taught me everything. I was getting nervous, pursuing Simone. Especially after she had pulled me in the midst of her voluptuous thighs. What began as a cinch of surreptitious lust had quickly yielded to uninhibited passion. I had assumed Simone's first dance with love was with a boy. She was like a medieval queen on her wedding night. We both cried. I began to think about Nadine. It was her fault. She had pushed me to the rim of ungodliness.

I must have had the worst luck in the world. A couple of months later, Simone told me she was pregnant. After she and I had been together that night, I moved out. I felt terrible about our indecorous affair. I knew she wanted to wait. Our urges had gotten the best of us. I didn't want it to happen again. We would now have to carry the burden of our indiscretion. I was already a dead-beat father of two little girls. There was no way I could afford to care for another child. Though I had no one to blame but myself, I blamed Nadine for my predicament. If she were around, I would not have been in this mess. Life was getting even more unforgiving, with no relief in sight. *"What do I do now*

Mamma?" Perhaps prayer was not enough. I hadn't gone to church in years. "Why me Lord?" I cried out to the heavens. Even though it was going to be a struggle, and I was hoping she would keep the baby, "Are you going through with it?" I asked. Simone hung up the phone. It might have been wicked of me to ask. But even the most corrupt heart fears the reproach of the one it loves. Its rebuke is like a silent killer. Children do not ask to be born. When they get here, the hands that are supposed to feed, must feed. The hearts that are called to love, must love. I wanted my life back. Not that it had been devoid of gloom. I knew, nevertheless, Nadine could fix it all. She had the keys to resurrect my life. She always made things better, just like Mamma. I was going back to my wife and kids. I would get my kids from Nadine's mom, get a job Upstate, and be with my wife. Life was going to be beautiful again.

CHAPTER SIX

I went Upstate, New York to find the girl of my dreams. I found her sitting at a desk in the school library. She was so lost in her book; she didn't realize I was sitting across from her. "Baby," I called out to her quietly.

"Jesus!" she screamed at the top of her voice.

"Are you all right?" this tall, rough looking guy, just like a football player came over to ask.

"I'm okay, I'm okay," Nadine told him, stretching her arms over her face to catch her breath.

"Is that your boyfriend?" I asked.

She looked as though she had seen a ghost.

"What are you doing here? And where have you been?" She asked.

I couldn't tell her I was with Simone; so, I lied. I told her I was back home all that time, to clear my head. Her parents were peeved at me, she said. They wanted to serve me with child support, but she stopped them.

"I knew you would be back," she scoffed.

"You know, Nadine, I almost forgot how beautiful you are."

She softly drew in her breath, her eyes gazing into mine. We stared at each other for a long time. What in the world had I been doing? My wife was utterly gorgeous and smart, as Well. She was the only one who could make my heart dance.

"Violin, I'm a different woman now...uh..." Nadine's voice dimmed as her words sputtered.

"Is everything okay with you?" a young woman, peering our way, probed.

"Yes, I'm fine," Nadine answered, shaking her head.

The lofty shelves surrounding us like two birds in a cage might have provoked the spiky haired young woman's curiosity. It must have looked as though Nadine and I were in a secret den. "Nadine, please forgive me. I'm sorry," I said, trying to reach for her hands.

I started to laugh at my own words. It sounded like something Daddy would say. I got on my knees and crawled in between Nadine's thighs. "I'm nothing without you," I told her, "Please let your husband in."

She did not utter a word. The almost soundless groaning coming out of her, bared her soul. I leaned closer and gently pressed my lips against hers. I felt the unburdening of heartfelt relief.

Though we weren't really divorced, Nadine agreed to rekindle our vows. Her parents hated me. They disowned her for taking me back. She told them she was grown enough to make her own choices. I felt terrible about them rejecting her. Then again, I was delighted she had finally freed herself from their iron grip. She would always be Daddy's little girl. As her husband, she was my woman. Her mom was hysterical when we went down to Brooklyn to pick up the girls. When we got to the house, she was sitting in a rocking chair, staring idly at the ceiling. "Mama," I went to hug her, trying to make amends. She didn't want me near her.

"You've taken my daughters from me," she said.

What about me? I kept thinking.

"Her dad was right, you know," she pressed with an unforgiving look.

While I understood her pain, my heart had its own heavy wound. Nadine was like my Savior from Hell. We both couldn't live without her.

"Mama, I have to do this for me," I told her.

She took out what looked like a damp beige cloth from the front pocket of her dress and patted her cheeks.

"I ain't your mamma," she said, her voice soaring with contempt.

Nadine stood inert at the center of the staircase. Her dad trailing not too far behind, each of my daughters at his side.

"It's okay, darling, your mother will be fine," he told Nadine.

"I can't take it; I can't take saying goodbye to my babies," Nadine's mom, sobbing, stood up and ran out the living room.

"Mom, please don't do this," Nadine ran after her.

"Maribel! Let the children go, I tell you," her father shouted behind them.

He put both of my daughters down.

"That's what a real man does," he said.

Still, he refused to shake my hands.

"We'll come back to visit," Nadine yelled out to her mother, who had walked back to the living room.

Her mother's eyes looked as though they had gone through many sleepless nights.

"It's time," Nadine handed me the keys to her car and told me to head out with the girls.

Watching Nadine and her father clinging to each other while walking out, it reminded me of me and Mamma. I felt like a thief, walking away with his own blood. As I waited outside with my daughters, Nadine's mom came running out.

"Let me say goodbye to my kids," she said, bidding each one farewell with a kiss.

Then, she battered my soul with a piercing insult.

"Some of you, Black men, disgust me," she muttered under her breath.

Nadine and I moved in with the twins in a small apartment, Upstate, New York. It wasn't too far from where she was going to school. The girls were now three and a half years old. We had to find day care for them. Nadine was still attending school, full time. I got a security job at a store nearby. It wasn't paying much. At night, and on the weekends, when Nadine was home, I worked a second job at a movie theater, doing the same thing. I wanted to take care of my family, making everything right again. It was a struggle, but life was good. A year later, Nadine graduated with a degree in political science. She was now on her way to law school. I surprised her on her graduation day. She had a huge beam on her face when she spotted her mom and dad in the crowded auditorium. When Nadine and I left to go Upstate, her mom seldom wanted to speak to us. She wanted me and Nadine to move back in the city, to which Nadine and I declined. Nadine's mom was so upset we had rebuffed her suggestion, she'd said, as long as Nadine was with me, Nadine would never amount to anything. The last time Nadine and I went to visit her parents with the kids, her mom told us not to expect her at Nadine's graduation. "There won't be one after this boy gives you another baby," she told Nadine. A week prior to the ceremony, I called her parents to share the good news. "What do you want?" her mother asked. When I told her Nadine was graduating, and I wanted her and her husband to come, "Alleluia! My son," she shouted. I could hear her soft tears. "Thank you, I love you," she said. A load had been lifted off my shoulders. It felt awesome hearing these words from Mama. I was her son again.

Nadine started law school the following year. Although she couldn't work long hours, she wanted a part time job to help me with the bills. Her mom wouldn't let her. Since Nadine couldn't get a full scholarship, her mother took out a loan to help her pay for school. Her cousin, Monique, came to live with us to help with the kids. She had relocated from England to the U.S. and was living with Nadine's parents. As a favor to Nadine's mom, Monique promised to stay for at least the first two years Nadine would be in law school. Before moving to England, Monique lived in Arizona with her husband. She left him after he had broken their marital vows. A splendid looking woman in her forties, Monique was thrilled to be back in the States. "England is great, but America is where I found love," she quipped. I enrolled in nursing school part time at a community college, while still working two jobs. Nadine and I hardly saw each other. She was proud of me, "You are a good man," she said. There were days, I wished things were different. Mamma, I'm sure was singing praises in Heaven. Her son had turned into a real man. Underneath it all, I was holding secrets. I never told Nadine about Simone, about her being pregnant with my child. I had reached out to Simone. She had given birth to a baby boy. She named him after me. I never wanted a son; not after what I saw Daddy do to Mamma. I was excited, nonetheless. That joy could not be shared with my wife. Nadine would leave me if she found out. Her mother would shell her with "I told you so," renderings. Twice a month, I would send Simone money for the baby. I knew hiding the truth from Nadine was wrong. A good husband takes good care of his family and builds his marriage on trust. That, I learned from Mamma, instilling in me what she never had. I couldn't do both. The guilt within me threatened to drive me insane; I fought it. I vowed to love Nadine for life. Married life, however, slowly started losing its appeal.

Monique worked part time during the middle of the day, while the girls were at school. She didn't really have any rest or leisure time. As she spent most of her time taking care of the kids. In the evenings, it was just her and Nadine in the house while I was either at work or school. She looked after the girls even when Nadine was around. Monique hardly complained. Even so, Nadine sensed she was getting a bit exhausted. She also began to develop a passion for hard liquor. Though I never had an obsessive taste for alcohol, it appeased my angst. Monique offered me a taste; it led to a winding road of forbidden passion. She was as gripping as the whiskey that had enticed my lips. It was just like the other stuff that started happening. A lot of it was beyond my control. It was getting difficult fighting whatever in me that was choking up my marital vows. It battled me so tirelessly; I could no longer resist its bait. It all started the day Nadine took the girls to visit her mother. Hell had uncovered the many hidden demons inside of me. Monique stayed back. She was going to finally enjoy a day all to herself. When I came home that night, she had a tall glass of who knows what in front of her. I couldn't turn down the toxic brew, nor the excitement she had to offer. We were both out of our minds. Our lips touched, then everything else followed. It had brought on a stream of affairs with other women. Some, I knew from school. Many others were spur of the moment escapades at the brothel house. I couldn't figure me out. I felt condemned. Yet I couldn't control what was happening. The thrill of it all was like a drug. Disgusted with my mulish ways, the longing was more intoxicating than any urges I had ever felt. It made me feel like a new man. With so much tension building up in me, I was no longer the prey of my own rage.

Things were about to become even more complicated. Nadine was pregnant again. We were about to have another girl. Nadine wasn't as flustered as I was. Although she wished it had happened after she was done with law school. "It's okay, thank God for another princess," she said. We would find a way. There is always a way, she urged. Simone, however, was beginning to fuss. The money I was sending was not enough. She had lost her job and was barely pulling through. I begged her not to tell Nadine. I needed more time. With a new baby on the way, life started to feel like an open grave. With so much on my mind, the bottle became my companion. I was turning into Daddy. Perhaps there was some truth to what he said, "Like father, like son." I had his blood. Mamma often said, she and Daddy were descendants of two different kinds of humans. She used to compare it to flowers. Daddy, she said, was as brazen as an angel's trumpet, while she was as delicate as baby's tears. Though there had been the frantic cry of a little boy inside of me, I was becoming like Daddy, like a profane trumpet of a fallen angel.

Monique could no longer hide her guilt. She told Nadine about us. It tore open the gates of hell. It broke Nadine's heart. It was like a sickness without a cure, I told her, begging for her forgiveness. She'd had enough of my vacillating excuses. I once had to confess. I had taking her to a basketball game at my school. My carnal indiscretions turned out to be the main event. Jazz, whom I thought of as my "Ebony rose," invited her friend, Monica, who happened to be a desk clerk at Nadine's law school. It started a freakish wave, nearly turning into a riot. Jazz knew I was married. When she discovered her friend Monica and I had our own closet affair, all four of us were uprooted from the gym. Jazz stoked Nadine's anger, seeing how composed Nadine was. "That's what happens when you're too busy and can't take care of your business at home," she'd told Nadine. I had gotten my wife ensnared in the middle of a fling fire. Both Jazz and Monica started bashing me with angry words. Nadine said it was the worst humiliation she had ever endured.

My marriage would have ended that day, had it not been for Monique pleading on my behalf. She told Nadine she had forgiven her husband many times, before finally deciding to call it quits. Now, we were both claiming to have gotten drunk. Later that same week, the day Nadine was graduating from law school, Simone called. She told Nadine I had a son. My marriage was over. Nadine swore to leave me for good this time. She was going back to live with her parents. She took my girls, along with her fancy degree, and said goodbye. Monique flew to Seattle to be with this guy she had met through a chat line. It was a slow waltz inside the gates of hell from that moment on. I had been so angry with Daddy; I never went back to visit him. Jessy and Josie didn't care if I was dead or alive. I once again felt alone and afraid. Nadine was not coming back. She sent me divorce papers a few days after she left. The one who provided comfort to my soul had left me to burn in hell.

After Nadine moved out, I would send her checks for my girls. She returned them. She didn't need my money, she said. I wished Simone could've felt what it's like to have your feet hanging above hot flames. Perhaps she did, trying to raise Violin Junior on her own. I blamed her, nonetheless. She had ruined my life and now wanted child support. I take care of my own, I told her. I would never allow my son to suffer. Anyhow, the feds came after me. Once Simone got them involved, I hated her even more. The law was treating me as if I was a "good for nothing" father. I wasn't. I loved my son. While I was furious with Simone, I desperately wanted to see Violin. He had just turned three and still did not know his dad. I flew out to *Cali* to see him. He looked a lot like Daddy. Simone wanted me to tell him I'm his dad. "What's your name?" he asked, after he had told me his name.

It took me quite a while to answer. "Well, son, my name is Violin," I told him.

He had a nervous grin on his face.

"Violin what? Violin what?" Simone prompted him to ask, his smile fading. Simone stood behind him, gently stroking his shoulders.

"My name is Violin Labonne," I answered, getting down on my knees. "Just like you," I said, his snicker coming back.

"Like me?" his face gleaming with a jumpy giggle.

"Yes, just like you," I told him.

He seemed lost, as if looking through me. He pulled his hands back and held on tightly to Simone.

"I told him his daddy's name," Simone said with tears. Violin Junior then turned to his mom, smuggling his face against her thighs.

"It's okay, sweetie. It's okay," she told him.

Holding my son for the first time, I had never felt so much anxiety about being a father. I worried a lot about him being a boy. I would have to teach him things I hadn't even yet figured out. When Sarah, my youngest girl was born, life welcomed her into a marriage in peril. Yet, it didn't frighten me as much.

"I'm scared, I don't know how to do this," I told Simone. I hated that she had named Violin Junior after me and gave him my family name.

"He's your first son, raise him to be a real man," Simone intoned. It sounded like an insult.

"It takes a man to raise a man," I lashed out.

"Sorry," she grunted, damning even more the anguish within me.

"Please, help me. I don't want to let you down, or any of my kids," I told her.

She took me into her arms and bowed my head over her shoulders, as Violin Junior looked on. At twenty-five years old, I struggled to finish nursing school. I'd promised Mamma, her son was going to be an attorney. I would defend people who had no one to turn to. Being a nurse, I hoped it would bring her a smile when she looked down. I was going to help save lives. Going up the stage graduation day, I felt abandoned. Even my own shadow seemed to have deserted me. Mamma's precious son, her prince, was now only a fairytale in my dreams. Everyone I'd ever loved had abandoned me.

———

The wall clock read half hour past midnight. I had broken into the home, not at all sure why I was there. I could hear my heart pounding inside my head. I moved like a ghost about the hallway. The house, dark and soundless, its deafening silence felt in my stomach. Suddenly, a clamor of loud clatter took over my head, a shrilling melody overhead. Startled, I ducked beneath the stark-naked, gloomy sky window. A warm breeze covered my head. Sprinting inside the room, then creeping in with springs under my feet, It felt extremely cold. As if the chill of death had made it home. The fleeting shadow of a woman with her top bare zipped past me. *Slug!* A huge explosion inside the house. It shook me. *"Oh my God, what have I done?"* Everything then spiraled out of control. The piercing shouts overshadowed the screams inside my head. The cold air littering my soul. My body now like an iceberg. I closed my eyes, to open them up again. "What are you doing?" Nadine cried out, hurtling her way past me. Patches of her hair slid through my hands. She raced out of the room.

"Life is not worth living without you," I shouted after her. She tripped and almost fell over the steps railing. I reached out with both hands for her to come to me. A terrified look on her face, "No, Violin! No!" she pushed my hands back. She got back up and took off running again. Nadine staggered down the stairway and ran out the front door. I ran after her.

"Don't leave me! Don't ever leave me! Nadine, NADINE!"

My frantic shouts had been trumped by the crushing blow of the car hitting her. "Oh Jesus!" almost gasping for air, I woke up with a sweltering fright. It was all a dream.

I turned to Simone. She had been encouraging me through many solemn nights, when I wished I didn't wake up from sleep. It would be understating to say she wasn't looking for love. She found the love that had for so long eluded her in me. She asked me to move in. A month later, we got married in front of a judge. I don't know why we did, getting married that is. It had Violin Junior doing cartwheels. He drew a picture of the three of us. Simone and I locking hands, with him in between us. He understood Mommy and Daddy were now husband and wife. "You love Mommy now?" he asked. I had a difficult time convincing myself this was about love. Simone was not like Nadine. She was much more forgiving. She was not going to stir up my guilt. It may have been the reason why she and I stayed together much longer than I thought we would. She said she had pushed the government to collect child support, out of fear I was going to abandon her and Violin Junior. Simone's dad walked out on his family and never looked back. Simone was in middle school at the time. Her mother died a year before Simone graduated from high school. She had been on her own since. Simone was a good woman, a great mother to my son. But after a while, we knew we had said our vows in vain. "I'm still looking for love," she said. It was painful to hear. We were married for a little over two years. "He will always be yours," she said. She kept Violin Junior, nonetheless.

With Nadine, Daddy, and now Simone out of my life, I moved back to where I belonged. I went back to

Brooklyn. I rented a small apartment not too far from where we used to live. Brooklyn was where I was loved. My place of mourning was also where Mamma had prayed a long time for me to come. Home, even in the midst of chaos, is still home. Daddy never wanted us to come. Not until we had all finished school. America, he said, would ruin us. As a child, I couldn't understand why he thought of America in such a way. He hated that he would have to spend the rest of his life in the "dungeon," as he often called America. Mamma said it was because no matter how hard Daddy worked, the fruit of his labor was never enough. Life in America, Mamma said, could turn anyone into a wolf. When I moved back to Brooklyn, I thought a lot about what Mr. Pierre-Louis had said about Daddy. How he once was a well-known schoolteacher back home. I wondered if it had fueled Daddy's resentment of America. Still, America would always be great, Mamma said. The land of opportunity was also the land of a second chance. That's all I wanted — another chance at life. I wanted to start over. Even with everything I had been through, life was still fighting to give me hope. My anger towards Daddy began to slip away. I missed hearing his voice. I wanted to be with my girls. I had not seen them since Nadine left. A week after I had been home, I drove to Nadine's house. The home had been sold; the new owner told me. "That sweet girl and her husband moved to Long Island," she said.

"Husband!" I yelled out in shock.

"Yes, child," she said, with a similar accent from people back home; "Nadine and the whole family moved with her lawyer husband, Bob."

My hands began to shake, violently. Beads of sweat slid down my face and whirled inside my mouth. My lips suddenly felt hot. They tasted bitter. I must have stood there for what seemed like hours without a word.

"You all right, Mister?" the silver-gray haired lady asked, as I brooded over her words.

"What's...uh, what's your name?" she then pointed her fingers at me with stuttering lips.

"My name is Violin," I answered.

She quickly pulled the screen door, locking it from the inside. Perhaps she did not realize the other exterior door was left ajar. I watched, as she ran towards the living room. "Oh my God! Jean-Claude, Jean-Claude!" she screamed out. "That nasty boy is here," she said to the bulky, fat stomach man rumbling down the steps. He ran past her and unlocked the screen door.

"Vagabond, don't you come here no more," he shouted.

I was now a monster in everyone's eyes.

CHAPTER SEVEN

I got a nursing job at a hospital in Brooklyn. Raging mad, trying to get over Nadine being with somebody else, I was on the verge of losing my mind. The walls were closing in. The tears wanted out. Yet despair in my soul echoed louder. When life threatens to rip you apart, fight, anyway you can, Mamma said. Although I no longer wanted to be with Simone, I hated being alone. And so, I got married again. Her name was Florence. She was not Nadine, but it was close. And it is only because Nadine was my first love. Florence was also a nurse. We met at the hospital while working a late-night shift. She made my soul dance. Though I loved Nadine, I couldn't always tell how much she loved me. With Florence, there wasn't a smudge of doubt. She loved me more than she had ever loved anybody else. That's what she told me one day. I believed her. Florence loved me just as much as Mamma did. I was the center of her world. She took care of my every need. "I will show you what a real woman feels like," she said. Florence may not have been the girl of my dreams; she, nonetheless, performed miracles, far beyond Nadine's reach. My lustful thirst was gone. I had no desire for anybody else. Florence was a beautiful looking woman. While she was a year shy of turning fifty; she dazzled me with the charm of a much younger woman. She had silky, dark olive skin. Her chest like a mountain of treasure. It comforted my sorrows. I was only twenty-seven. Yet, our great difference in age didn't seem to matter. Florence shook my world. She was everything I had ever wanted in a woman. With Florence, I became a different man. "Fight for your kids," Florence told me. She knew about my son. She wanted me to see my girls. I had a daughter who scarcely knew me. Sarah was only a couple of months old when Nadine took her and my twin girls away. It didn't matter that Nadine did not want my money. A real man, Florence said, would find a way.

Though she had been divorced twice, Florence knew how to take care of a man. Her first husband couldn't keep up with her in the bedroom. So, she left him. Her second husband was extremely jealous. He didn't allow her to have any friends and would follow her everywhere. The possessive man had turned into an abusive husband. I was much more pleasant, Florence said. Much more levelheaded than her previous husband. He must have been a fool, I told her. Being married to a woman like her was like joining hips with the queen of an earthly paradise. The woman was breathtaking. Her good looks gave me even more reasons to worship her. She would turn a lot of heads when we go out. But she was *my* woman. At home, I was her king. When we were at work, Florence would set my table in the cafeteria as though it were home. Her caring heart, the quarry of unflattering looks, bled for me. The only thing Mamma told me to ever take from a woman is her love. And even that isn't free. You must give it back, twice over, she said. I didn't need anything but Florence's love. Yet, she gave me what more than warms a man's heart. She surrendered every inch of her body, to the depth of her soul. I couldn't wait to show Nadine the type of woman I had ushered into my life.

After close to three years not seeing my daughters, I finally reached out to Nadine. The first time I went to visit my girls, I brought Florence with me. Nadine and her husband lived in a lavish gated home in Long Island. Her parents had relocated to Florida. It was just Nadine, the girls, and her husband in the house. Nadine had allowed us to visit after Florence and I threatened to take her to court. Driving towards the home after going through the security gate, I saw my twin girls standing outside. They both looked nervous. Noelle, the first to be born, held her sister's hand, her face bowed to the ground. Nya stared at the car the whole time. When we had reached the end of the driveway, after what seemed like miles of unending roads, "They know who you are," Florence calmly let out. "Daddy," Nya seemed to have edged out of her lips. I was unsure if any words came out. She walked slowly towards the car. The weight of the world had been lifted off my shoulders. My feet felt heavy getting out of the car. "Hi, Dad," Nya mumbled with a smile. I wrapped my hands around her. She closed her eyes and blew out hasty breaths. Florence let herself out; Nya waved at her with an awkward gaze. Her gaping lashes narrowed intensely.

"Is that your new wife?" Noelle asked, pushing her sister aside to grab hold of me. "She doesn't look that old like Mommy said," she puckered her lips. Florence didn't look too amused. I had told Nadine Florence was a seasoned woman, not old. Although she didn't say a word, the look on Florence's face had condemned me. When we made it inside the house, Nadine's husband was the first to greet us. He was a tall, good-looking guy. He had blonde hair and hoary eyes. Nadine didn't tell me she had married a white man.

"What a fine thing," Florence muffled under her breath.

"You want him too?" I let out, feeling my jaw muscles stiffen.

It wasn't because of what Florence said. Bob was holding my baby girl. She was calling him Dad.

"Who's this man, Daddy?" she asked.

"Mommy's friend," he said to her.

I lost it. My mind shifted into another world. The melody of madness playing in my head, my heart pounded even faster with each angry breath. "Give me my little girl," I burst out in anger. "And he's not your dad, I am!" I screamed at Sarah. I came so close to punching Bob. But he was still holding my little princess. Sarah started to cry. She looked so much like Mamma. She had our slinky eyes and the same bushy eyebrows. As I was about to pull her away, Nadine came running down the steps.

"Stop it, Violin," she howled at me. She sent the older girls to their rooms and told Bob to take Sarah out to the playground.

"Why is she calling him, Daddy?" I yelled out, shouting at Nadine.

She asked Florence if she didn't mind waiting out on the playground with Bob while we talked in private.

"You're wrong for doing this," Florence told her.

I may have been a fool, not fighting hard enough to see my kids. Yet not a day went by without me thinking about them, especially Sarah.

"I didn't think you were coming back for them," Nadine cut through me.

"You're the one who pushed me away," I told her.

She lowered her voice, as if she didn't want anyone to hear. "You've hurt me deeply; let us not dwell on the past," She said. She pleaded with me to allow her time to tell our daughter the truth. Sarah was only three. She still had a fragile mind Nadine said. I told her she had better let Sarah know soon or I would tell her.

"Violin, please don't make this difficult for me," she said.

Lost in her gaze; I was forced to swallow the thought of what could have been. My anger wavering in submission, "I'm not trying to make things difficult. I just want my daughter to know who I am," I told her.

"I'll handle it, trust me," she replied.

"Are you okay, hon?" Bob shouted from the patio.

"Yes, sweetie, give us a few more minutes," Nadine answered.

Seeing Nadine again, sent butterflies down my stomach. She looked more beautiful than I had remembered.

"You look different," I said to her.

"So do you," she said. "Florence must be taking good care of you," she added with a faint giggle.

"Why him?" I asked.

"He loves me," she countered with a whisper.

Unsure of what came over me. "But I love you too," the words fluttered out. "You're not the only one with a broken heart," I told her.

She stood undeterred, quietly staring into my eyes. "Please don't do this," she said.

During the drive back home, Florence didn't say much. The few words she let off sent chills throughout my body, speechless, my heart racing. "After everything I have done for you," she leaned her head back, "you don't look at me like that."

Had she read my thoughts? I had been trying my best not to show it; the rush of excitement consuming me when I saw Nadine. It was awfully intense. Though we were listening to rhythm and blues on the radio, the music had lost its rhythm. It was all blues. When we got home, Florence took a bath, got dressed, and said she was going out.

"You are a beautiful woman; no one can ever take your place," I told her.

"I'm just your play toy," she replied.

Florence went out and didn't return home until dawn. While she was gone, I couldn't stop thinking about Nadine. When Florence returned, however, I lusted after her. "Where did you go?" I asked. She wouldn't answer. Resentment began to settle in. It was the same rage that ran through me when I saw Nadine with her new husband. It felt like a sacrilegious blend of love and hate. Florence reeked of cigar when she came back. She refused to tell me where she had been. It was almost getting to the point of no return. I was losing my grip on her. And so, I pressed again. "Where did you go?"

"Someone else appreciates what you don't," was her answer.

My question did not return void. It had incited a sinful craving. She knew what she was doing. "Don't make me ask again."

She laughed, inviting more the thirst of her seductive snare. "What, you want me now," she said, removing her top. I couldn't even breathe right. Her lure had gotten me to surrender.

"Tell me you love me...say it again...say it again," Florence charged, hovering over me. She had to put her hands over my mouth to help muffle my screams.

"Learn to respect a real woman," she said. The beast within me ensnared back into her cage.

Things were never the same between me and Florence. I began to despise her. She didn't take care of me the way she had been, thereafter. She and I would drive to work and return home without much being said. I cooked her dinner most nights. She would eat alone, then head straight to bed. The more she ignored me, the more I lusted after her. "I want out," she said a few weeks later. I scuffled with her not to leave. She had gathered her clothes in a suitcase and was on her way out the door. I wouldn't let her leave. I held on to her wrists, firmly clutching them with both hands. "Please, don't do this," I pleaded with her. There was a struggle within me. It was like the sun fighting the rain. I wanted to strike her. The urge burning like wildfire inside of me.

"Are you going to hit me? You look like a demon," she said.

"Please, don't do this," I begged her again. The heinous thoughts wanted to come out. They were at the tip of my tongue. *How dare she? Over my dead body she will walk away.* I knew I was at fault. But why was she leaving me? Was she going to be with another man? Florence heard me confessing my love to Nadine on the phone. I told her it was nothing more than a playful exchange with the mother of my children. She sensed my heart pulling away. I still couldn't let her leave. Who was going to take care of me? My mind started to race like a man possessed. I was begging her to stay, yet also wanted to scold her with my fist. Nadine was nothing more than an old flame; I tried to convince her.

"Come to me; don't do this," I pleaded.

She refused to allow me near her. I lunged at her, pushing her against the wall. She almost got knocked to the ground.

"My goodness, Violin! You're scaring me; I've never seen you like this," she cried out.

I was trembling with fear. I wouldn't give in to the rage. I couldn't do it; Florence left. I was an insane man, she said. I hadn't lost my mind. It wasn't fair of love to tease, then throw me into the pit.

"You'll do fine without me," Florence said.

Why couldn't she understand? I needed her. Besides, I had kept my hands cleaned. Not entirely faultless, but free of wrath. It was like a gentle torture, like tussling with myself in the mirror, fighting madness inside my head. My mind telling me to *tear, tear, tear*. As if my spirit had turned against its own flesh. The voices came from nowhere. They prattled loudly, their chatter without end. I didn't split the rose; yet I couldn't be left alone. I ran after Florence. She was standing near the bus stop across the street. Her back resting against her car door. She was shedding tears. Both of her hands covered her face. Her cry sounded like the weeping of a battered woman.

"Please, love, please forgive me. This is all love has taught me," I said, falling to my knees. I pleaded for her to come back.

"Say yes," a young lady walking by shouted.

Florence cried even louder.

"I can't live without you," I said, grabbing her by the waist. "Look at me. I'm at your feet looking like a fool. I have no one to go to. No one but you. I love you. How can you think Nadine is the one I love?" I told her.

Florence came back, but what we once shared never did. Our intimate moments were now dispassionate flings between jaded lovers. There wasn't nothing left of me to love, but hurt, envy, and rage. Desolate thoughts filled my heart. I loved Florence, but I couldn't stand seeing Nadine with another man. I couldn't hide the rage. I took it out on the bottle. It was the only way to conceal the pain. Florence was beyond fed-up, sickened by my breath of despair. She nagged me about drinking too much. Yet the bottle kept me from putting my hands on her. Many days, my fury arose. And I thought, this is it. This will be the day when evil defeats me. You look for ways to stop. But you can't. It is a temperamental beast. Spontaneous when it wishes to unleash its venom. I refused to allow its might to rule me. I willed myself out of my toxic taste bud. The day I got sober, another demon came out of hiding to torment my life. "See, you wanted me back, but you're not attracted to me anymore," Florence complained. I was. Loving her the way she needed to be loved, however, would bring out its own devil from hell. Whenever we would go visit my kids, seeing Nadine, I would return home lusting after Florence. It would be the only time my bottled-up anger would find pleasure in her. "Why do you now love me this way?" she asked. What do men know? I tried to hide my sin. A woman knows. Her wit guides her like a goddess' wisdom. Florence had even accused me of calling out Nadine's name. I denied it, of course. But who knows what can come out of a man in the heat of passion? Especially one with a troubled soul. The instinct of a woman, Mamma used to say, is as powerful as her love. So is a woman's scorn I found out. I came home one day, the house bare, staring at me. I thought we had been robbed; not even our wedding pictures were on the wall. I tried to get a hold of Florence on her pager. She never returned my calls. There was no way she was going to walk out on me without saying anything. Even my clothes were gone. I called the police. When the officers arrived, one of them went to inspect our bedroom. When he came out, he was holding several white sheets of paper, wrapped around a dollar bill. "What is that?" I asked. I must have overlooked them when I went in the room.

"Sir, you've not been robbed," the officer said, holding a slight grin. "You've been dumped," he said, as he handed me the sheets of paper. It was a divorce notice, with a note attached. *"Here's what you have left,"* Florence wrote. She apparently cleaned out our bank accounts.

"Wait, there's more," the officer said.

By now, so humiliated, I didn't know how much more I could take. Buried inside the divorce papers, a lewd photograph of Florence with another man, exposed. With that, she had buried me to the ground. She took her love away, along with my dignity.

CHAPTER EIGHT

I started to think, perhaps Mama was right. Not my mamma, but Nadine's mom. Men like me were no-good, she'd said. It stung like a sword at my back. Her words had nearly broken everything in me. They had me questioning love—self-love. Mamma taught me how to love, but hate, self-loathing, was teaching me a lot I hadn't known about love. The darker you are, the less it seems to want you at its sight. It reviles you, as though you spurred on its fear of midnight darkness. Nadine was the darkest one in her family. They all had yellow apple skin. "You're very handsome for a dark-skinned boy," Nadine's mother once told me. Perhaps, her repulsion of some of us, Black men, had more to do with our darkish shades. I had always been proud of who I am. Heeding Nadine's mom disheartening words, I carried my blackness as a life sentence. There were so many things Mamma didn't tell me. A shade too dark for some, I was also a beast without a heart. Still, Nadine loved me. Yet, she as well seemed to have parted with blackness. The tide of anger swamping me was not allowing me to breathe. It had me dangling my soul into another man's world. "I don't think I could ever marry another Black man; they're all the same," Nadine's mother would barter. It had been said so often; I began to wonder if it was Nadine's reason for marrying a white man. She always did whatever she could to make her parents happy. Perhaps I was to blame. Woeful memories of me may have left Nadine doubting her own kind. What were my kids going to think of me? "I am every bit the man your husband is," I told Nadine. Although at times, I wasn't so sure. It was because of what Mamma told me. Our skin color had different roots. If you were a doctor, or a lawyer, then its roots did not matter much. They would almost disappear. I thought my star-crossed roots had faded away, once Nadine told me she loved me. Nevertheless, I was not like Bob. He was a lawyer and had good roots.

When Nadine finally told Sarah, Bob was not her dad, she cried the entire night. I felt horrible. I just wanted her to love me. Perhaps it was too much, too soon. She asked her mom if I was going to move in. Bob was furious. He'd told Nadine, I only insisted on my daughter knowing the truth because he's white. To allow any man to claim your child as his, is like forfeiting your blood to nourish the soil of another man's yard. I couldn't have cared less what Bob thought. When I would visit my kids, he made me feel as though I was less of a man than he was. "Where did you go to school again?" he would ask, as if he had forgotten the answer. "I went to a community college," I would say to him. Somehow, the words would always stammer out of my lips. "Oh yes, I did forget," he would laugh, or stare at me with a smirk. It's bad enough; I had to find out from one of my daughters, he had made partner at the firm. I told him his fancy law degree didn't bother me. But it did. I wasn't impressed, I told Noelle. "I don't care if he's a big shot lawyer. I don't want to hear any of you girls calling him Daddy," I said to her. Nadine thought it was wrong of me, feeding our daughter such a venomous hate. "You need to stop being so bitter," she said. I was teaching Noelle about life. About the world, just like Mamma had taught me. She died young. I had to fend off everything life threw at me on my own. Having good roots didn't automatically turn someone into a saint, I told my girls. "Learn from your uncle Jessy," I told them. He looked like an Adonis god and was Doctor of Psychology. Yet, he was as wicked as can be. I was about to tell them how Jessy beat up on his wife and kids; Nadine stopped me. "You've gone too far now," she snapped. Nevertheless, like Mamma taught me, I told my girls, to be a worthy soul, one has to have a god's brain and an angel's heart.

It upset me that Nadine didn't want me to tell our daughters about the demons in our family. They would eventually find out, I told her. She didn't even want me to talk to them about race; what Blackness once meant in America. Perhaps she was afraid to tell them the real reason she had married Bob. Then again, why couldn't she love a white man? I was still at my wits end, trying to figure out why I hated him so much. Surely, Bob was enjoying his opulent life with my kids and the love of my life, adorning his castle. He had everything I had ever wanted. A love gone astray had not been so kind. Nadine hadn't told my daughters why she and I divorced. Telling them the truth, she said, would have them think of me as a scumbag. It was such a deplorable thing to hear. It had slayed me with a dagger in the heart.

A year after Florence and I divorced, I met Priscilla. She was one of the attorneys trying to get Daddy release early on parole. "You must have a good soul, wanting to be the monster's PD," I told her. She laughed. "Interesting choice of words, we're all fighting our own demons" she answered. Priscilla and a couple of her associates decided to help after Daddy told them about me. "I hear you have an angel's heart," she said. She edged out each word as if she was already convinced. Neither Jessy, nor Josie wanted to help. They told Priscilla they despised Daddy. So, he was counting on me to shell out a few good words on his behalf. "We're hopeful the parole board is as forgiving as you are," one of Priscilla's associates asserted. I felt somewhat torn. Part of me wanted to see Daddy out early. Then again, I blamed him for everything that was happening to me. Daddy was in poor health, Priscilla said. Finally, after nine and a half years in hell, Daddy was about to be a free man. "Parole is a get out of jail card, only if you follow the rules," Priscilla told him. Nonetheless, Daddy would no longer be in hell. They told the parole board he would be living with me. Daddy never made it home. He died of heart failure a week before he was scheduled to be released.

It was such a strange twist of fate. Daddy told me he had discovered faith in prison. Even though prison had been like hell. Not too many people attended the funeral. Simone wanted to come, but later changed her mind. Since her mother died, she couldn't handle being near dead people. Nadine showed up with my daughters and her husband. Jessy and Josie did not come to pay their last respect. They told Priscilla; they had already buried Daddy long ago. Thankfully, I wasn't there alone. Priscilla stood at my side throughout the entire service. "Is that your new girlfriend?" both Noelle and Nya asked. Priscilla told them, she was just a friend.

Nadine thought there was much more to our companionship. She refused to believe Priscilla was nothing more than an acquaintance. "The girl wants you, Violin," She squealed relentlessly in my ear. "I'm a woman; I know these things," she said. When she found out Priscilla was a lawyer, I could tell she was a tad bit jealous. "So, we're competing now?" Nadine asked. It wasn't my plan, initially. But once these words came out of her mouth, I made a bitter vow that Priscilla would be more than just a friend. Still, there was more behind Nadine's words than simply an ex-wife's playful contempt of ranks. She didn't say it; yet seeing Priscilla was a White woman seemed to have rattled her nerves. It might have been a sinister thought; yet I saw the resentful spirit of rivalry in her. It's no wonder she thought I was trying to compete. Even her husband started to show me respect. Thinking Priscilla and I were dating, he greeted me with slobbering admiration. Priscilla was an Ivy League graduate, while Bob was not. I made sure to tell him.

"It's always good to see you, Violin," Bob greeted me and Priscilla. He wanted to know when we would be coming over for dinner. This was the America Mamma warned me about. The one she abhorred. It was the same, back home. Most strove to showcase their roots. But in America, it could still get cutoff with a bigoted sword. I had struggled with my roots in the face of self-loathing and rejection. But now, they didn't seem to matter.

"Am I now part of the family?" Priscilla asked, as we were leaving the funeral home. It was too tempting, she said, not to snoop on Nadine's grudging speech. Timidly gazing into her pearly eyes, "My wish, your choice," I answered, before asking her out on a date.

"Your daughters are beautiful," she said.

I felt like an idiot.

"I guess, I'm out of my league," I told her.

"No, not at all," she replied, grabbing my hand. My chest was getting warm. The dazzling, flawless skinned blonde, agreed to go out with me. So yet again, my life was about to take another turn.

With Daddy gone, I only had my kids to worry about. They were getting older. I didn't want them to think I was a drifter. When Daddy took Mamma away, I was left with despair as friend. I lived with rage. Now that he had gone to be with Mamma, he left me with more grief. My children would never know their grandparents. They would only know how beautiful Mamma was through pictures. They would never get to know Mamma's love or take pleasure in her graceful steps, when her heart was cheerful. Mamma loved to dance. But only when her sorrows weren't eating at her heart. The day of my birthday, when I was turning fourteen, Mamma came back to help me celebrate. She was dancing with me in my head. Her face beaming with joy. Daddy didn't know what was going on. "What's wrong with you?" he asked. He saw me idly swaying to a lonesome dance. I didn't tell him it was because of Mamma. It would make his blood run cold. I wasn't afraid. Her ghost had come back to take out the guilt from my heart. Mamma and I danced, just like we used to most Sunday afternoons after church. As if Mamma's ghost had swayed Daddy to join in; he got up and put on a vinyl of Mamma's favorite song. It must have made her angry. Mamma's spirit went away as soon as the song began to play. She showed me the scars on the back of her head. "I'm slayed. He gave it to me; he did this to me," she screamed. Her spirit flew away with the wind of the melody. Once again, Daddy had taken away the joy inside of me.

So many times, I wished the stones could be turned over. My kids only saw their grandfather in death. I couldn't figure out what to tell them about why Daddy was in prison. Nadine told the twins, Daddy had stabbed someone in self-defense. I didn't want to take my girls to see him. Who knows how much in him, they would think lived in me. Before Daddy claimed to have found religion, there was no love in him. He said he loved me. His love, however, felt more like repulsion. "You're a gift," he said. I never felt like one. I wanted to fly away, fleeing my doleful silhouette. It made me feel like a pariah. "He belongs to us," Mamma said. But not his heart. I started baring the guilt, nonetheless. The twins wished they had met Daddy before he died. I couldn't stand lying to them. Mamma got killed at the hands of a monster, I told Noelle and Nya. I never told them who the monster was. They would grow up hating me, if they found out I had helped conceal the murder of their grandmother. There were times, I thought my sin was worse than Daddy's. I hated him even more after his death. He said he had found peace. Yet, where would I find comfort. When Mamma would take me to church, most of the time, I didn't have a clue what the preacher was saying. I had a lot of questions; Mamma always did her best to help me understand. She would say to me, "God can save any soul." With so much hatred growing in me, it scared me to think, how would my heart be judged?

On our first date, Priscilla suggested we meet up for lunch at this trendy Caribbean café in the city. On a cold winter evening, with the blast of frigid air scouring her face, she greeted me with a cold kiss on the steps of the train station. I had offered to drive, but Priscilla wanted to ride the train. She was that type of girl—classy, yet humble. It blew my mind that she had agreed to go out with me. Her sleek, golden hair pulled back, and her eyes looking like the heavenly sky. "C'mon, hurry," she shouted as the train was pulling in. Sitting next to her, my mind felt at peace, without worries.

"Why are you so quiet," she asked, as I perhaps appeared lost in my own world.

There was always this serene, melancholic air, consuming me whenever I would ride the train. The smell of chafing steel, and the melody of squealing tracks, were both endearing and gloomy. "I'm fine, nothing is wrong," I told Priscilla.

"Well, it's time for us to get to know each other," she said.

She reminded me so much of Nadine. A sweet girl—eager, vibrant, with an indelible smile, as an Ivy League graduate, I expected her to be a snob, but she wasn't. It was because of her father, she said. He had also been a public defender, but he had retired. Her father didn't think the justice system always treated everyone equally. He'd fought to help those without a voice. He served those whom justice alienated for most of his career. Her mother, Priscilla said, was a schoolteacher. She taught for over twenty years at one of the worst public schools in Brooklyn. Her mother had vowed to help troubled urban kids. The more Priscilla spoke about her parents, the more I started to think it was going to be a match made in heaven. Mamma always told me, God could heal a broken heart. Healing, she said, would sometimes come as a butterfly. I had this longing to belong to something, to someone. To help me escape my darkness. I saw the butterfly in Priscilla's eyes. She was only a few years older than me. And yet, at thirty-five, Priscilla had already accomplished so much. She was an extremely driven young woman. A former prosecutor, she wanted the world in her hands. She admitted to "switching to the other side of the pendulum" for a good cause. She hoped to one day run for office in our district. When asked, why she wanted to be district attorney, "Why not?" she answered.

At the café, the moment Priscilla and I walked in, we were drawing too much attention. We sat down to order our drinks; already, I started feeling annoyed. "What's wrong?" she asked.

"You're a White woman; that's what's wrong." I sensed she had been taken aback by my answer.

"Why did you ask me out, then?" she leered at me.

Priscilla wasn't the problem. We appeared to be everyone's topic of conversation at the restaurant.

"Really, that's what worries you?" Priscilla arched her lips with a loud snicker. I told her the whispers and funny looks bothered me.

"Baby, you have a lot to learn, then," she let out with a city girl sneer.

The way she uttered baby, everything about her seemed real. I was convinced she had no hidden contempt towards my dark body. I was feeling her. Yet, for some reason, it still felt a little awkward. There weren't that many couples like us around. And if there were, did any of them struggle with my unease. I wanted to run. My own people were looking at me with pondering eyes. I couldn't. I felt at home.

"Is it a crime for you to love me?" Priscilla asked.

Love! I couldn't even look at her eyes.

"Look at me, honey; you have gorgeous skin, beautiful dark skin, and a smile to kill for. That's what I see."

They could have thrown stones at me then; I wouldn't have cared. Priscilla went on to explain a view of the world, which had me pasted to my seat. She compared her mission to defend the voiceless, to children who have been ripped apart by abuse, especially children of color. Though children may grow up in the same household, the one who has suffered at the hands of the predator will have anguish for life. Trauma has invaded the souls of many of these innocent children, Priscilla asserted with tense breath, her mascara running behind her tears. "Let me finish, Violin," she said when I offered her a glass of water.

Priscilla likened the plight of these children to systemic racism. "These children have been violated," she said. "Yet, we ask them, why can't you be like your brother, *Johnny*? Or your sister, *Jill*. But their feet are still shackled by fear."

She paused for a much-needed breath.

"Their hands bound by inauspicious justice. And their minds, still handcuffed by the strain of the great injustice," Priscilla said, wiping colorful tears on her face. "You understand?"

I nod.

"With me, Violin, it is not as much about the forgotten sin, as it is about justice. At the end of their sad stories, these beleaguered young spirits can't stand tall. In contrast to their unbound brothers and sisters, the picture may not look as pristine. The ink in their minds has dried up, while the one holding the pen gets to finish the story. Then, the predator returns as prosecutor, judge, and jury. That's why they need people like me."

I started thinking, Mamma wasn't lying about God sending helpers as butterflies.

Not too long after our first date, I proposed to Priscilla. After three failed marriages, this was it for me. I was deathly afraid she was going to turn me down. We had only been dating for a few months. And a guy like me was not the one her family expected her to bring home. One, who could possibly bring discomfort at the dinner table. Priscilla agreed to spend the rest of her life as my bride. She only dated lawyers ever since she got out of law school. I worried her parents would reject me. Driving to their home, Downtown Brooklyn, I was amazed at how excited Priscilla was about me meeting them. Her parents lived in a modest two-bedroom apartment. The neighborhood was unassuming at best. It surprised me there were still many white folks living in these apartment complexes. Where I lived, there weren't too many around. Mr. Alberto was the only one left. He was a nice man. A long-standing member of the community, he liked to call himself. He and his wife would often throw these extravagant Fourth of July parties. His whole family would come, and everyone would have a good time. Mr. Alberto didn't want to leave. He refused to abandon the neighborhood. There was still life in its blood, he said. Others had disappeared, as though they were running away from having their names engraved on a tombstone. It wasn't so with Mr. Alberto. Death was everywhere, he said. And so was life. So long as our neighborhood had life, he would breathe its air with us. Sadly, Mr. Alberto eventually moved out. He'd told Mamma, there was no such a thing as perfect love. It was a sad day when he left. Mr. Alberto used to encourage me to study hard and not to worry so much about being an immigrant. "We're all immigrants, we're all one," he used to tell me. His heart could no longer bear to live as one. Priscilla's parents, nevertheless, still called a reviled inner-city neighborhood their home.

Meeting Priscilla's parents for the first time, "Have a seat," her father muttered over a thick cloud, smoking a large cigar. He was a hefty, tall man, with boxy shoulders. "Are you a lawyer?" he asked.

"Not yet," I answered, feeling somewhat embarrassed about not being one.

"Good," he said, "then you will treat her right."

Most of the men Priscilla brought home, according to her father, were "a bunch of skirt chasers." When Priscilla's mother inquired about my family, I told her a fairytale of a boyhood dream; unaware, Priscilla had already told her about Daddy. "There is something you need to know," Priscilla's mother said as she was giving me a tour of the apartment. She looked like the type of woman who once could turn a man's spine into gelatin. One, who wouldn't have been afraid to carry the strongest man in the world on her back. She wasn't nearly as tall as her husband, but she walked as though she were. Her eyes stood tall., sky-blue, abounding with confidence, yet kind. I was afraid to find out what was going to come out of her.

"Every family hides its own ugly truth," Priscilla's mother confessed. She wanted to be the one to tell me about their own family secret. I started perspiring a bit. Was Priscilla's father just like Daddy? "Forgive Priscilla for not telling you," she said. She was about to reveal a truth from the den of hell. Their only son was serving life in prison for killing his wife. A cloud of disgust covered me. Was Priscilla with me out of pity?

"Why didn't you tell me about your brother?" I asked Priscilla when we got back to her apartment. I told her my story was not a crutch for rehab. She admitted to not telling me for the same reason I wasn't so quick to tell everyone about Daddy. She felt ashamed and angry. She knew her mother would end up telling me. I felt like a reclamation project to help amend her guilty conscience. She swore she wanted to marry me because she loved me. I felt betrayed. I almost broke off the engagement.

"You're all the same," I let slip.

"I'm going to pretend I didn't hear that," she lashed out at me, telling me how appalled she was with my endless self-pity.

I wasn't in need of a great white savior, I told her. I went on and on; lost in a longwinded speech.

"So, it's not real love because I'm white?" she asked, peeling away at my ignorant pride. "And if you're referring to the 'Great White Hope,' I'm not it. Send me to Hell for trying to help, Violin. But things are different now," she wiped her cheeks.

"Are they?" I asked.

We were sitting next to each other on the couch; yet it felt as if there was an entrenched chasm between us.

"I breathe air just like you do. I bleed like you do. I am not God. We all need one another. Even Dr. King marched with some of us," she stooped down in front of me, letting her hair out, locking her hands into mine. "So, you see, hon, you're wrong about me," she said, her eyes as soothing as the calm sea.

It was happening again; whatever in her that stirred every part of me. I was speechless, not a word would come out. My unsympathetic monologue feeling like angry, hot air.

"I'm sorry you feel this way, but I love you," she said.

"Do you really love me?" I asked, "You know, I mean, really?" I was fumbling for words.

"I adore you," she answered.

I was all together angry, though no longer sure at what; yet feeling on top of the world, thinking that I shouldn't be. "I need you," I told Priscilla. The flames behind her raged through the fireplace as if at Hell's door. The wood burning like scattered ashes. "Everything about you is beautiful," I stumbled over my words, lurching to give her a kiss. If anyone needed to apologize, it was me. I had been the one pretending. I wanted to get back at Nadine. My bitter motive had been deceived, outridden by its own scheme. Mamma often said, there was no greater love than that of a Black woman. With Priscilla, I found out, the comfort of life could also be found between the breasts of a White woman.

I fell in love again. "I feel guilty loving you," I told Priscilla, lying next to her. Love had prospered beyond the fright of my reluctant heart.

"What I feel for you sees no color," she said, gently running her finger like an engraved heart on my bare chest. Love, in me, was being carved out by someone whom I never envisioned could invade my blackness, my darkened soul.

"I shouldn't," I said.

"I want you to," she held me close.

Rain started to fall. A thundering flash of lightening nudged our bodies even closer. The warmth of her skin sent chills through me. I had been drifting through an unending road. A lonesome path filled with shameless cravings. Florence, I thought I loved. She was all *woman*. Priscilla was just as much a tantalizing queen. She took hold of the monster inside of me and put it to sleep.

Eight months later, Priscilla and I were meeting at the altar. We released three doves the evening of our wedding. One for Mamma, one for Daddy, and one for Priscilla's sister in-law. We got married on Priscilla's birthday. It was a couple of weeks before Christmas. Violin Junior, and Sarah, my little princess, both served as ring bearers. My twin daughters were also part of the bridal party. They walked down the aisle as princesses. Nadine offered me and Priscilla her best wishes. She, nonetheless, appeared to be on edge throughout the wedding ceremony. I had never seen her look so sad. Noelle told me her mom hadn't been feeling well. Standing at the altar, I imagined how different life could've been. With each step before Priscilla's father released my bride, I could see Nadine fidgeting in her seat. She put on her dark shades as Priscilla was being ushered into my hands.

"Smile baby," Priscilla spoke softly. I could hear my own voice telling me to "breathe, breathe, and breathe." Priscilla looked as restless as a mourning dove. It felt a lot like my first time, raw and innocent. And perhaps, it felt that way because I had never exchanged vows walking down the aisle. It was my first time getting married at a church. While Priscilla and I shared the same faith, it was a hassle trying to get a cleric to marry us in church. Her father wanted us to get married at the cathedral where he attended church. The priest interrogated me with the ire of a judge. He might as well had asked me for a signed confession.

"Have you been married before?" he asked.

"Yes," I replied.

"How many times?" he asked.

I lied. "Just once," I told him.

"Father, he's not telling the whole truth," Priscilla interjected.

She and I nearly got into a huge blowup inside the church, if not for the priest interrupting our shouting match. I had to apologize to the priest for our heated words. He was an honorable man. The bloodcurdling inquiry was part of Church doctrine, he said. Although none of my previous marriages had been at a church, being that it was my fourth time getting hitched, the priest was concerned. His tiresome enquiries had me feeling so ashamed, I bolted. There were too many questions. Too much about me to find out. It felt as if, God Himself, was punishing me for Daddy's sins. The curse of his beatings haunted me at the doorsteps of God's house. "Am I that repulsive?" I asked the priest, after he repeatedly questioned my motive for wanting to marry again.

Even the pastor at the church we got married made me feel as though my feet were dangling in Hell. Pastor Jenkins used to live on our block. When Mamma and I would walk past his house, he would invite us to church. "Jesus will be coming back soon," he would say to us. "I know," Mamma would answer. She then would tell him, Jesus was in her heart. Priscilla and I went to visit Pastor Jenkins, thinking he would have no qualms in marrying us. His condemnation was as damning as the Priest's reproach. He wanted me to go through extensive counseling after I had opened my heart to him. If Priscilla and I continued to live without his blessing, I told Pastor Jenkins, the church would have to carry the burden of our wrenched union. "Perhaps, God is trying to tell you something," he said. I asked him if he thought God would forever be angry with me. He had a puzzling look on his face. "I don't blame you for thinking this way, but divorce should not be taken lightly," he said. I thought about Mamma; all the beatings she wanted to run from. All the humiliations she had to endure; and wondered whether she would have ever left Daddy. Mamma would never disobey God. Then again, being with Daddy was like living in Hell. "Would God have wanted her to remain in hell?" I asked Pastor Jenkins, after telling him what had happened to Mamma. He finally relented and agreed to marry us in church.

A month before the wedding, I made a vow to change my life. Pastor Jenkins prayed with me. Kneeling beside me at the altar, he told God to steer me away from my own will. As he was praying, he put his hand over my head. He then started speaking in tongues. He covered my head with a stronger grip and began to shed tears.

"Why the tears, Pastor Jenkins?" I asked. He wept some more, crying so clamorously, he started to scare me.

"Son, be strong," his voice dimming, "there is a legion of them inside of you."

Them? I hadn't told Pastor Jenkins everything. How could he hear what was in my head? He stood up to pray over me. The voices began to laugh. Thank goodness Priscilla wasn't around. There was so much shame in me; I was too mortified to tell Pastor Jenkins.

Priscilla and I spent our honeymoon in Paris. She was amazed, seeing me fluently speaking French. She sensed that I had been modest in my delivery and now was eager to charm her. I wanted so much to impress Priscilla; it drove her nuts. "There's no need for you to go out of your way to show that you love me," she said, "I'm yours." I was scared as heck. Tired of what it feels like to lose the one you love. Our first night as husband and wife, Priscilla and I talked until the dawn of morning. After hours and hours of heart bonding talks, I pulled the cover over our heads and prayed that my sinful lust wouldn't return. It had overpowered my flesh, putting an end to my blessed union with Nadine. I swore not to ever let it happen again. My vow so daunting, it emasculated me. I was fearful of my own flesh. Throughout our honeymoon, my fear had hindered my ferocity to handle Priscilla's curves. She had led me beyond the borders of ecstasy. I now seemed to be utterly purged of carnal desire. Love, devoid of heartfelt wildfire games is not complete, Florence taught me. I was either going to be an extraordinarily loving husband or a savage lover. I couldn't be both. I would have to go on pretending. "Don't be silly, of course I'm still attracted to you," I told Priscilla. I only pursued her once. We spent most of our time drinking red wine and cuddling under the sheets. "You're scaring me," she said. Love had brought me to my knees.

CHAPTER NINE

Priscilla never made me feel like I wasn't good enough. And yet, her shadow of prominence was always around. After we got married, Priscilla and I wanted a fresh start. We thought about moving to Long Island, but Priscilla wanted to stay in Brooklyn. I moved into her brownstone apartment, not too far from where her parents lived. I told Priscilla, in a few years, we needed to buy a bigger home. I wanted a house with a large backyard. I was tired of living in apartments. She thought it was silly of me since we already had a home. Priscilla owned the apartment, but I felt closed in. For some reason, living in building apartments made me feel as if I was in prison. "How can you know what prison is really like if you have never been in one?" Priscilla asked. "Oh shoot, never mind," she quickly sighed. I hated when some of her colleagues were at the house. I sat at the table, lost in my own world. They all must have thought I was a blithering idiot. I hardly ever let out a word. I would listen, watching their swaggering lips grow even more presumptuous with each word. They were full of bluster. The way some of them stared me down would have one thinking I was a felon. Priscilla had to ask one of them to leave one night. He was one of those big-headed, loud mouths defense attorneys, whom she worked with at the courthouse. "Are you still pushing meds?" he asked. We all pretended not to hear. "No med errors now, or you'll need us to bail you out," he said, laughing out loud. Everyone thought it was funny. Priscilla and I weren't laughing. Some of her colleagues blamed it on him having too much to drink. Except for James, another one of Priscilla's associates. He said it was an outpouring of jealousy. The loutish attorney had asked Priscilla out to dinner. He knew she was married. Priscilla turned him down.

James was a good kid. He had too much of a boyish look to be the "Kick-ass" attorney Priscilla tagged him to be. The first time I saw him, I knew he looked familiar. I could not recall where we had met. He remembered me, however. He and I had the same English class our senior year in high school. He asked about Nadine and started joking about prom night. The news had gotten out about what Nadine and I did that night.

"I thought you would have married that girl," he said.

"She's the love of his life," Priscilla chimed in with a mocking chuckle.

When I told James, Nadine and I were indeed married at one time, and she was the mother of my three beautiful girls, he nearly dropped to the floor. He then patted me on the back. "You're a lucky son of a gun," he said, "having married another beautiful girl like Priscilla," raising his thump.

"No, I'm the lucky one," Priscilla said to him, softly drumming my chest with her hands. Thank God she did. She had doused the scorching envy running through my blood.

When James and I began to talk in private, he shared some things, which pared me like a slaughtered beast. Many of Priscilla's colleagues, he said, were upset she had married me. I was "a loafer" in their eyes. Rumor had it that I had at least six children, with six different mothers. And I was not taking care of them. When I asked him if Priscilla was aware of what was being said, "Who knows," he answered, shrugging his shoulders. The slighting remarks always came out, James said, when Priscilla was not around. "I'm sure worse is said when I'm not there," James confessed. Many at the office were outraged, Priscilla married a man of such unaspiring stature. I asked James if he thought "unaspiring" meant "Black man." He laughed,

"What do you think?" he asked. I was hurt but not angry. It's hard to get bigotry out of someone's heart, Mamma told me. When I told Priscilla about the despicable chatter, "I know," she said, "My walls have ears."

I told Priscilla It was time for me to return to school. I was going back to get a law degree. She reckoned, helping to save lives as a nurse should be rewarding enough. It wasn't. I always had to work twice as hard as everybody else. "The world does not like me," I told Priscilla. Being an immigrant, and dark as night, trying to pursue the great American dream had a far-reaching lethal grip. I started from nowhere. And where I sought to end up, did not want me at its sight.

"It's not entirely your fault," Priscilla avowed. "You've done well for yourself," she said.

It wasn't enough.

"I need to be treated more with respect," I told her.

She grunted with a soft giggle. "Respect! Here, you make your own way. And if it's not good enough for anybody else, who cares," she countered.

Back home, not too many people were fond of America. It is a land that ravages the soul, many believed. Yet, it was where they all craved to come, to help harvest their wealth and stature. Many had done it, Mamma said. They traveled abroad, worked hard, and fought like hell to keep their dignity. "Why is that?" I remember asking Mamma. She looked at me with bone-chilling fear in her eyes.

"America is the land of the survival of the fittest, honey," Mamma said.

I didn't understand survival of the fittest, but it sounded like a bad thing. "So, you do whatever you can to make it work?" I asked Mamma.

"Oh yes, sweetie, but ah…" she started humming.

"But what, Mamma? But what?"

She lowered the fire on top of the stove and took off her discolored apron. "Sit down, sit down," Mamma rushed me to a chair and knelt in front of me. "Honey, Black folks have to break down the walls, before they can get respect in this country," she said.

Things weren't much different back home. The most revered were either doctors or lawyers. Many had given up their souls in the struggle for success. Although the hope of making it in the land of the free, and home of the brave, was not what initially brought me to America, "Watch me climb to greatness," I told Priscilla.

"Most would weep of joy, having what you have," she said.

Still, I felt like a failure, lacking prestige.

"Watch me do it," I told her. I vowed to one day preside over a court room.

"A judge!" Priscilla shouted with a chuckle.

"Why not? In the land of the free, everybody worships freedom, especially freedom of achievement. Why not be great, why not be all you can be in America," I told Priscilla. "If James did it, why can't I do it?" I said, pounding the words out.

"But that's exactly the problem, isn't it?" Priscilla asserted. "Why do you have to be like him," she said. "Why not be happy with yourself as you are?"

I waited patiently as she spoke.

"Why do you want the DA's Job?" I then asked.

"Well, that's different. I mean, I want to help...Oh, forget it, Violin," she sounded annoyed.

It was what America had taught me. In the great land, one had to strive for more; strive to be the best. I was going to be so great; the world would forget my roots ever existed.

"I am the son of Violine, the offspring of a great woman. One, who battled the world with her scars hidden within," I declared.

Priscilla wrapped her arms around me.

"You are awesome, just as you are. Slow down some, love," she said, laughing hysterically. Even the voices joined in the laughter.

My passion for success awoke a desire to return to school. Mustering enough willpower to do it, however, had my resolve doubting in vain. When I moved in with Priscilla in her condo, I offered to help with the mortgage. Going to school full time, I wouldn't be able to help as much. Priscilla earned enough to cover the bills on her own. It didn't matter that she was earning a decent living as a lawyer. I was her husband. A man had to take good care of his wife, Mamma said. I worried about my kids. Nadine was okay with me going back to school. She told me to give the kids' allowance to Simone. It didn't feel right. I didn't want Bob to think his money alone was raising my kids. Nadine wasn't working as much since Bob made partner. So, I did what any good father would do. I worked full time at the hospital at night and went to school in the morning. Priscilla was not at all pleased with me not being home. She offered to send Nadine money every month for my girls. I wouldn't let her. It made me feel as though I wasn't a real man. She was proud of me, nonetheless. She worried we wouldn't be spending enough time together. She wanted children. "You need to be home for us to make babies," she said. Both, Pride, and love required sacrifice, I told her

Married for the fourth time, I was once again a new man. Our second Christmas day as husband and wife, Priscila and I had my kids over for a big feast. It was the first time I had all of them with me on a holiday. My girls were so excited, meeting their brother for the first time. Sarah followed him everywhere around the house. "Violin, Violin," she constantly screeched out, annoying everyone with her never-ending chant. She wasn't so little anymore, but she was still my favorite baby girl. I never told her she was. Yet she knew it. In my mind, I loved my children equally. There was something about Sarah that drew me closer to her. She once told me she wanted to be just like me when she grows up. I was afraid to ask what exactly she wanted to be. She and Violin Junior were close in age. So, my son often asked, why is it that I treated Sarah like a baby, and not him. "You love her more," he said. When Priscilla asked him why he thought I didn't love him the same. "Daddy is a lot nicer to Sarah," Violin Junior told her. My heart grew faint, hearing these words come out of him. I felt the same way about Daddy. It stayed with me even after he died. I told Violin Junior, because Sarah is a girl, she needed to be protected. My twin daughters didn't see it that way. They were now in high school. They thought of themselves as tough girls.

"Strong girls don't need protection; we got our own backs," Nya blurted out.

It surprised me when she said it. Nya was always the quiet one.

"Don't boys need protection, too?" Violin Junior asked.

"Of course, they do," I told him. Girls, I said, had to be cared for like princesses.

"What about a prince, who protects the prince, Daddy?" Violin Junior asked.

My inside beginning to turn numb. *Who is it that looks out for a prince?*

"The king, isn't it?" Priscilla answered, as if she read my thoughts.

I was cared for by a queen, I thought to myself, Just like Daddy. He didn't really know his dad. They met for the first time when my grandmother, Daddy's mom, was in her death bed. Daddy was ten years old at the time. He didn't feel a thing, he said, seeing my grandfather. It was the last time they saw each other. Daddy had to fetch for himself since. "Yes, a king and queen look after the prince," I told my son. All the while thinking, the queen destined to protect me was sent early to her grave.

I finally decided it was time to share the horrible truth with my kids. The awful secret about Mamma and Daddy. I knew the time would come when I would have to tell them. Waiting too long, or not telling them at all, would later cause a whole lot of sorrows. Besides, a hidden truth does not stay buried for too long, Nadine and Simone would say to me. It was up to me to tell the kids, they both said. Nadine even hinted for me to tell them while they were with me. She thought it was about time. Christmas season was not the most appropriate occasion, Priscilla feared.

"It's cruel of you; you're going to ruin their Christmas," she said.

No matter how horrid the truth, my children needed to know. It would almost be like a sin not to tell them.

"You're going to regret it," Priscilla argued, once again.

The callous monster was the hands which fed me, then took life from me. My children would have to know about the world. How ruthless it can be, even towards children. Mamma died around this time of the year. The jingling chimes of Christmas day had been savagely taken away since my youthful years. Life had been forbidding, even in the most joyful season of the year. And so, a few days after Christmas, with all four of my kids seated in front of me, and Priscilla at my side, I shared the gruesome truth about our family. I told them how Mamma died, how Daddy shoved her to her death. He couldn't control his anger, I told them. While Priscilla went along with it, she was still filled with outrage. Sharing the grisly tale, she said, was like wheeling a blade in front of my kids. It was a good thing, finally laying bare our family secret. It turned out to be a blessing. What I was about to hear from my kids, however, was anything but sacred. It trampled my bones like withered shafts. "Is that why I get angry all the time?" Violin Junior asked. He didn't get in trouble at school. But sometimes, he felt like fighting everybody, he said. The wave of painful memories had just begun.

"I have something to tell you, Daddy," Sarah sputtered out, her breath heavy and her eyes on the verge of darting out. She had a frightened look on her face. The type of look children display when they sense oncoming wrath. My twin daughters were trying to stop her from speaking. They yelled at her to be quiet. My little princess struggling to get the words out. Her baby doll face, almost turning bloody red.

"What is it you have to tell us, honey?" Priscilla asked.

"Oh my God! You're going to get us in trouble," Noelle shouted.

"We have to tell Daddy," Sarah yelled back.

All three of my girls were now pouring out tears. The twins had their hands pressed against their lips, their arms shaking, afraid to speak.

"Tell me, now!" I said, shouting at both of them, feeling a father's burning rage storming out.

"Bob, Daddy uh…Bob," Nya struggled with the words, trying to tell me. "Bob hits on Mommy, too," she finally let out.

There are times when one wakes up from a nightmare, only to go back to sleep, then wake up again without the memory of the nightmarish dream. I had hoped that my nightmare would never come back. And yet, as it faded away, the roots of its rancor sprung to life again. It was like fighting death. Its snare, relentless. If there was one thought in my mind after what my daughters told me, it was to take Bob to the abyss with me. He would be going six feet under, while my soul would be standing in line for an unescapable voyage to Hell. "Pray for me to get back in one piece," I told Priscilla.

Driving back to Nadine's house with my girls, I had not a clue how I was going to react. My son stayed back with Priscilla. Violin Junior, we discovered, had been trying to cope with his own demons. It took me back to when I was a kid back home. I didn't know it then, but the demons had already entered me, taken me on as friend. "Swallow your tears," I remember them singing to me on Mother's Day. At school that same week, all the students had to wear roses, woven into their uniform to celebrate Mother's Day. The roses were only for those students whose mothers were still alive. If your mother was deceased, one had to wear violet or black. I wore purple and black. I went to school with the color of my spirit on my chest. "What is wrong with you?" the teacher asked. "Why do you have that color on?" She frowned.

Mrs. Theodore was good friends with Aunt Clarissa. She knew Mamma wasn't dead. "You're a strange child," Mrs. Theodore lashed out at me. I didn't think I was. What was strange, I told her, was hearing Mamma's tears every night in my sleep. Her screams just as loud, even when my eyes refused to give in to the dark. What was strange, was the soundless beat downs echoing, though no one could hear them. They rang inside my head like drums. Thumping blows, coming from far away, yet running through my body like a gush of violent wind.

"You see, Madame, I wake up each morning with a broken heart, an invisible black eye, and an unseen cloak over me to help hide my bruises," I said to Mrs. Theodore. She said I wasn't normal. "Whose fault is that?" I asked. Violin Junior may not have yet been fighting the same crippling demons; cursed would be the day they made his body home. The evil tormenting him threatened to devour his helpless soul with the same depraved mind. My son was no match for these dancing spirits. It was just a matter of time before he hears them calling his name.

"Don't you cause any trouble now," Priscilla had said on my way to Nadine's house. She didn't understand. She couldn't come to grips with the resentful spirit coming out of a deeply wounded heart. Nadine was no longer my wife, but she was still the mother of my children. I prayed for the rage within me to go away; it wouldn't leave me. The girls had reassured Nadine they wouldn't tell. All three had fear in their eyes. A few weeks after Florence and I first came up to visit them; they saw Bob hitting their mother. I was almost certain he had made it an atrocious habit. They would hear their mom screaming in her bedroom. "Daddy, is Bob a monster like Grandpa?" Sarah asked. She lit a torch inside of me. She would overhear Bob telling Nadine, he was going to kill her.

"When we get inside, y'all need to go directly to your rooms," I ordered my girls, clobbering the front door with both fists.

Nadine slowly opened the door. "Come on in, Violin," she greeted me with a nervous grin.

"Where is Bob?" I asked.

He wasn't home, she said. She gave each one of the girls a kiss and watched them career up the steps.

"Is something wrong?" Nadine asked.

From the way her eyes gaped at me, she, without a doubt, sensed an unsettling war waging in me. Her pretty face buried under an agonizing stare, "Violin, I'm talking to you. Why are you back so soon?"

My silence mirrored my mood. Perhaps wanting to keep under wraps what she knew was in me, "I knew you would come. He's not here, and he won't be coming back soon."

Nadine was a smart girl. Like a knight, wielding a heart of decay, I did come to her rescue. My vengeful heart galloped to save her, riding a wave of dark thoughts. She must have surmised, with me sharing the horrid story of their grandparents, It would frighten the children enough to tell me. Especially Sarah, she always got into trouble with her sisters for talking too much.

"I'm sorry, Violin. I told them not to tell. But…uh…I'm so sorry."

"You don't have to apologize," I told her.

I knew better than to add to her misery. Her coldblooded husband was the one who needed to beg for mercy.

"Was it Sarah?" Nadine asked, ushering me to a seat in the living room.

"You know it; she's a news anchor in training."

I was about to tell her it wasn't the best way for me to find out. But then, I thought of Mamma. When a woman is trampled beneath the sleeves of love, she would say, coherent thoughts sometimes elude her. The longing to "will" love, becomes her weakest armor. Self-preservation abandons her mind. And only leaves room for her to catch her breath.

"Why not walk out the door?" I asked Mamma.

"Everyone must think it should be easy to run away," she'd said.

Daddy walked in right after. "What is this boy asking you?" he asked, his face narrowing with wrath.

"A thoughtful question, which begs for a prudent answer," Mamma replied.

"Can we come out now," Sarah shouted from the top of the steps. "Daddy, I heard you calling Mommy, baby," she said.

"What did I tell you about snooping?" Nadine scolded her.

She quickly pedaled her tiny feet, running to me.

"Why didn't Mamma leave Grandpa?" Sarah asked.

"That's it! Go back to your room and stay there!" Nadine yelled at her.

"She talks too damn much," Noelle grumbled about her little sister's wild lips.

Both she and Nya now wanted to come down. Nadine was getting more irritated. The house sounding like a raucous caravan, Nadine insisted on the girls going back to their rooms. I told her the kids and I didn't get to finish our talk. I had been so angry, all I wanted to do was deal with Bob. He was going to be late coming home, Nadine told me.

"Well, it's a family get-together then," I let off.

"Hmm! Did you say family?" Sarah screeched out, grinning with sarcasm. She stoked the flames of hell again when we all sat down.

"Daddy," she asked, "Why didn't the police arrest you too?"

My mind running wild, spinning out of control, about to raise hell. But how could I rebuke an evil craft out of my hands. "Yes, Sarah. I should have. I did a terrible thing," I told her. She was so angry with me for lying to the police about how Mamma died.

Bob was visiting his parents out of town. Nadine planned it that way. She told him she was feeling too sick to tag along. "How many times?" I asked, after the girls had gone back to their rooms. Nadine stared coldly into my eyes and disrobed. There were bruises all over her back. Some of them purple, and others, black. It took me several painful breaths before uttering a word. And when I did attempt to shell out my anger, the words faltered under my breath. The fire in me burned with disgust. "I'm sorry," I said, helping her put back on her blouse. The human heart is a powerful thing. It can love and hate all at once. With a seething rage inside of me, my heart ached to rekindle a lost love. The lure of the appalling stripes covering Nadine, unyielding, enticing me to love a savagely battered and bruised body. Her beauty radiating even more. We sat next to each other on the couch. Nadine looked peaceful, laying her head on my chest. My heart pounded with pitiless rage.

"I'm going to kill him."

"Violin, please, don't talk like that," Nadine sulked, her voice ringing inside my chest.

It was her sole reason for not telling me. The only time the kids saw Bob hit her, he had completely lost it. She told the kids it was because he was drunk and didn't know what he was doing. He wasn't. Bob was distraught. Nadine discovered his secret. He was infertile. I felt bad for him. But even worse for Nadine. For having to swallow the burden of Bob's umbrage.

"Let it be the last time he hits you," I told Nadine. I no longer wanted my kids around him.

"He's my husband," she raised her head, eying me with a slight sneer, our lips inches apart.

My girls were so excited, but my wife wasn't. It started snowing heavily. The drive from Long Island to Brooklyn would have been too risky. I decided to stay the night. Priscilla wanted to pick me up after telling her that Bob was out of town visiting family. Even with our truck, she had to turn back. Violin Junior was still up, crying in the car. "He's upset; we are both worrying about you. We need you home," Priscilla commanded. I told Violin Junior, I would see him in the morning before he leaves. Simone was picking him up the following day to spend the New Year with him. Priscilla wanted me to stay at a hotel. The closest one miles away, I told her, she should trust me enough to know, Nadine and I would never sleep in the same bed. She was livid. I was supposed to come back ahead of the storm. "You have to trust me," I told her once more as we said good night.

"Sure," she answered. There was no denying the harsh sound of jealous anger in her voice.

We were like a family again. The twins recalled some of the good times we spent, Upstate. They reminisced about living in that "tiny place." It may have been a "four corner" apartment building; nonetheless, we were proud to be the Labonnes. We were the perfect family then. The girls stayed up and played board games almost the entire night. We all wished Violin Junior was with us. I thought a lot about Priscilla. Yet, it felt as if I was home. Sarah was the first to go to sleep. She was so exhausted after running around the house with her sisters' pompons, pretending to be a cheerleader. Around two in the morning, the twins went to bed. Nadine looked cheerful. The gloomy face she wore most of the day had disappeared into the night. She and I spent most of the night on the couch talking, after the girls had gone to bed. Her body was still hurting from the vicious blows. "He's a savage," I told her. I had gone to the car to get a few medical supplies, hoping to ease some of

Nadine's pain. Dabbing her back with ointment, her bra slid down, revealing more disgusting wounds. There were black and blue welts on her breasts. Feeling my stomach throbbing under the veiled silence in the room, "Can I?" I asked.

"Yes," she shook her head as I was about to withdraw my hand.

I gently rubbed the cream on her breasts. The radio humming softly, stringing along a melancholic tune. The lyrics to the song rang loudly in my ears. We both glanced at each other, quietly heeding every word.

"Together Again, by Skye Davis," the vee-jay calmly uttered, as the track was ending. There was no tranquility of souls, however, where Nadine and I sat. We were drowning in restless tension.

"Do you remember prom night?" I asked, running my fingers over the gut-wrenching wounds.

"My best night ever," Nadine answered.

"Mine, as well," I replied, feeling my hands shivering. She leaned over to kiss me. I took her lips within mine. Her face damped from weeping. We closed our eyes and fell asleep on the couch, locking arms.

The next morning, even if the roads hadn't been cleared, I had to leave. I didn't want the girls to get the wrong impression. I'd promised Violin Junior that I would see him before he leaves. And Priscilla, the way she sounded on the phone, it wouldn't have surprised me if she was drafting her own divorce papers. On the way home, I had a lot to think about. The roads were plowed, but it still was going to take some time to get home. Kissing Nadine felt like kissing Priscilla. That was not a good thing. "Jesus," I cried out, again and again. I don't know why it kept coming out of my mouth. It felt as though I had committed a terrible sin. Nadine stirred up a rush of sorrowful rage in me. Although I hadn't slept with her, she made my inside dance like a butterfly. I couldn't stop thinking about the scars on her back and all over her breasts. My heart shook with bitterness. How dared Bob put his paws on the woman I love? Having so many welts covering her breasts, like rims of tattoos, not even animals get tortured like that. I wanted to crush Bob with my fists. Suddenly, there was a police siren behind me.

"Sir, you've just ran a red light," the officer stated with a commanding voice after he had gotten out of the police cruiser.

"I'm sorry, officer. I have a lot on my mind," I answered.

"Have you been drinking?" he asked.

"You're kidding me, right?" I replied out of frustration. I handed the officer my license and registration. He then ordered me out of the car.

"Officer, I just want to go home," I said to him.

"Get out the car!" he shouted.

"Please, officer, let me go home. I have to go see my son," I begged him again.

"I'm asking you one more time to exit the vehicle," he said.

"Why are you getting all bent out of shape over a red light?"

I was so angry getting out of the car, I accidentally shoved the car door onto him. By the time I heard the ear-shattering blast of his gun, I was already on the ground. He shot me in the leg. I didn't even see when he drew his weapon.

I was in a hospital bed with my arms in cuffs, asking myself, how did I get there? I could have been dead. "He works here," everyone kept saying to the officers standing guard outside my door. The nurses were in shock, seeing me being escorted by the police. They wanted to know how I ended up with a bullet lodged in my leg. The officers kept a muzzle over their lips. They couldn't talk about the incident they told the nurses. So, someone had to do it. I told them what had occurred. At least, what I thought happened.

"They're going to charge you with assaulting an officer," Priscilla roared out as soon as she entered the room. She stormed in there like a woman on a death mission. Priscilla was so angry; she didn't even care to listen to my side of the story. "Learn to keep your mouth shut," she said. She wasn't happy to learn I had told the nurses about the incident. I asked her if she thought they were really going to press charges. "What do you think?" she answered with a smirk. "You hot-tempered idiot, didn't you hear me the first time," she stared me down with gaping eyes.

I reached for her to come to me. She shoved my hand back.

"Come on! Priscilla, don't do this," I told her.

She repeated the hellish words, once again.

"You're being charged for freaking assaulting an officer," she spewed out each word with fire in her eyes.

Assault! I couldn't believe what I was hearing. it was an accident. There was a lot on my mind, and I wasn't thinking straight.

"So, what got you all worked up?" She asked, her flaming eyes coming back to life.

Playing superman to an ex-lover, she thought, was what got me in trouble.

"Nadine is a big girl. She knows what to do. Next time, you'll know better. And you better pray they don't send you away for a long time," Priscilla cautioned.

A nurse came in and asked if she was my wife. Priscilla ignored her, as if she was ashamed her husband was now a crook. If our marriage wasn't on life support after spending the night out with Nadine, what then came out of my mouth, threatened to bury it for good.

"Your parents wished someone could've stopped your brother from beating a woman to death."

"Talk shit, you need me now," She said with a repugnant stare.

I spent the New Year chained to a hospital bed. No matter how much I pleaded with Priscilla to forgive my distasteful words regarding her brother, she refused to let it go. "If I were you, I would be extremely cautious with me," she said. She still wouldn't come near me. I kept thinking, how did I get myself into this mess? What had fueled my anger had more to do with a childhood nightmare than my affection for a battered ex-wife. Did anyone care to know what was going through my fractured soul? Nadine and my girls seemed to have been the only ones compassionate enough to find out. When she and the girls heard what had happened to me; they wanted to come to the hospital. I told Nadine not to come. Not with the way Priscilla was acting. She was kind enough to work it out with the officers to allow me to call my girls. Still, it was a safe bet a riot would have erupted. "I'm so sorry, Violin; It's all my fault," Nadine told me, sobbing on the phone. She was more sympathetic of my grave error than Priscilla had been. I had overly reacted without thinking. The twins didn't say much. They were thankful I wasn't dead. They thought the cop who shot me might have been a bigot. I didn't want them to think that way.

"The policeman needs to go to jail," Sarah unleashed. Daddy's little princess was furious. I was partly to blame for what happened. I didn't want my kids to think cops were bad. Albeit it was the way most Black kids in my old neighborhood thought of them. Mr. Alberto used to tell me, bad cops have nothing to do with the badge. The heart donning blue, he said, should be what we impeach. Mr. Alberto had two brothers who were police officers, living in Bensonhurst; a southwest section of Brooklyn, also called "Little Italy." It was home to a lot of men and women in blue.

Once, there were huge riots in Bensonhurst. Black folks were outraged over the murder of a Black teen. Though the police had nothing to do with the killing, I was terrified. I loved Brooklyn, but its streets weren't kind to us, Black men. My twin daughters had heard at school about another incident. A terrible thing had happened to this immigrant man at the hands of the police. There were once again uprisings in New York City, amidst alleged cover-ups by the police. The only "Wall of Blue" that exists, Mr. Alberto affirmed, is to help protect and serve. Who will be left to protect us, he said, if we're constantly beating down the men in blue?

Mr. Alberto thought police officers were like soldiers, worthy of honor. He couldn't understand why so many people in our building abhorred the police. Most of them understood the cops were there to help. Nevertheless, I heard of some dreadful stories about the police when I came to America. Mr. Leonard, who used to live in our building, and whose family was from the South, recounted endless Black enclaves, brutally raided by the police. "That was all in the past," Mr. Alberto admitted. Perhaps the thoughts of those horrific memories still haunted a lot of Black folks, I told him. I figured then, why many Black people and police officers hold distrust of one another. Some Blacks are scared stiff of Blues; while some Blues feel unappreciated by Blacks. It leaves all of us with bruised hearts, bleeding the same color. "Who knows?" I told my daughters; although the officer shot me unnecessarily, I might have reacted the same way if I were in his shoes. He had every right to return home whole to his wife and kids. And I had every right not to get shot. Both of our lives mattered.

I told Simone not to tell Violin Junior. I didn't want him to think I was a criminal. Though she didn't say it, Sarah was beginning to think of me as a fraud. She wanted to know why I seemed to always get in trouble with the police. There was no way she could understand that I was still struggling. The frightened little boy had turned into a terrified man. Mamma taught me love. Daddy filled my heart with hate. Everything in between, I had to learn on my own. I was scared. I've always been afraid. Even the dark of night freaked me out. Its shades haunted me even in the light of day. Only Mamma knew that. She figured out a lot about me. Things, I was afraid to tell her. She would sometimes sing them to me when telling stories. Especially the one about the angry little boy. He had a softness to him, she said. But inside of him, lived hell, which she doubted the world would ever understand.

Little boy, little boy, little boy, she'd sang. *When the voices in your head return. Say goodbye, say goodbye, say goodbye to them.* Mamma always ended the last verse, crying. And I always listened to it, angry. She would then talk to the Spirits of the air, praying to them with her hands over me.

"He cries in the deserted midnight darkness and thinks no one hears him. But Lord, you know best. A mother's love never rests. Her heart never goes to sleep," Mamma cried out, both of us on our knees. "*Please, don't cry Mamma; God won't let them come back,*" I wept in silence. The song in my head burning.

Both Priscilla and James went to bat for me. They sought the help of the district attorney and pleaded for leniency. They said I would only get probation if I pleaded guilty to a lesser charge. The officer told them he was in fear for his life. He had every right to defend himself, thinking I was trying to attack him. But I wasn't. His perception along with my honest mistake could have turned deadly. I didn't think it was fair for me to serve even a day of probation. But it was the best deal the DA would offer. It would only be for six months. I still thought it was an unjust punishment. I felt like a felon. I had promised Mamma, her youngest son would never be a criminal. I was both the victim and the offender.

After nearly two weeks bound to a hospital bed, I was still a prisoner at home. Reporting to my probation officer was the least of my problems. Priscilla was acting like a scorned woman. She blamed me for getting shot, and said she had to beg for favors from people she detested. She could've fooled me. She and the DA were the best of friends at one time. I knew she worried what she had feared the most had happened.

"Did you sleep with her?" she finally asked.

I told her nothing happened. I wasn't so sure she believed me.

"Did you do anything with her?" she was hell-bent on discovering the unimpeded truth.

I had to collect my thoughts, almost forgetting I was being questioned by a former prosecuting attorney. There was no way she was going to get the truth out of me. A Kiss is just a kiss, but not when one's marital lips are locked up with that of an ex-lover. Once divorced, a wise woman told me, one may search for love again and never find it. But if you do, don't ever allow your new love to be haunted by the faded spirit of a former lover.

"Nothing happened between us," I reassured Priscilla. I still thought about Nadine. While on probation, it hindered me from doing anything to Bob. Wanting to slaughter him with my bare hands had gotten me in a whole heap of trouble. Priscilla didn't want me anywhere near him. She was afraid he would get me locked up. I confronted him, nonetheless. He tried to ridicule me when I called. I fought hard not to be hostile towards him. He baited me mercilessly. I told him I would have him arrested if he ever put his hands on Nadine again. He didn't seem to care. "What else can you do?" he asked. Anything else out of my mouth would have been considered a threat. Our conversation then ended.

A few weeks later, Nadine told me things were going well. She perhaps was being careful with her words, not wanting me to spend the rest of my life behind bars. Even so, I told my girls to keep an eye on her. While Bob hadn't hit her, he started drinking a whole lot, Nadine told me. I wanted my kids out of his house. And worried about Nadine. Once my probation was over, I told Priscilla we would have to speak with Nadine about moving my girls. I wanted them to come live with me. Priscilla thought it was a bit too extreme. "Give it more time," she said. The thought of me sleeping with Nadine flooding her mind, Priscilla's resentful spirit haunted me like hell. More and more, she began to complain about everything. She didn't want me anywhere near Nadine. She worried so much about what Bob would do to me. I was too involved in his private affairs, she said. It surprised me to hear that from her. Bob would do it again. It was just a matter of time. I learned from Daddy, the empty bottle usually makes it worse. The more he drank, the more the demons came out of him. As the mother of my children, I worried about Nadine's safety.

"You want her to leave her husband?" Priscilla glanced peevishly at me. All Bob needed, she said, was counseling to help with his inner demons.

"He's going to kill her one day," I told her. I didn't want my kids around to see it. Nor did I want them to lose their mom.

"C'mon, it's not just about your kids," Priscilla raged. She accused me of not yet quenching Nadine's fire inside of me. I had; the flames burning were being fueled by singing spirits.

Priscilla's sudden late evenings at work started fueling my own jealousy. The abrupt change in schedule initially did not bother me. It escalated to a point, however, I could no longer tolerate. She claimed there were some things she couldn't do at home.

"You obviously think I'm a fool," I told her. Whatever it was, I'm sure had nothing to do with legal ethics. Assuredly, I didn't know anything about how court attorneys do business. But the thought of Priscilla being with another man had my blood wildly running afraid. I couldn't stand to think she had betrayed our vows. Priscilla staying out late every night in the company of scavenging men had me so furious; my anger piled up, drifting within, as though scattered along the banks of an angry river, wanting to swim with sharks. James told me he wasn't part of the nightly meetings. I figured he was covering for Priscilla. He, as well, started behaving differently. He and I had gone to school together and sat in the same classroom. We always treated each other with respect. Even after he and I had crossed paths again, he never failed to look at me as his equal. Now, I didn't know what to think. He would avoid talking to me. And even seemed nervous to look at me in the eyes. As if I suddenly wasn't good enough, or able to stand as tall as he could reach.

The evil cycle had me feeling like a dark horse. It is shameful enough when a man looks down on another. But for a Black man to look up and see repulsion in the eyes of his brother. It cripples the soul. It crushes your spirit like nothing else can. James lit up a bitter spirit in me, enough to send me to Hell.

Priscilla was ashamed of me. And so was James. He finally admitted it when I pressed him to tell me the truth. Pretty much everyone around the office had been giving Priscilla a hard time after the incident with the officer. "That's what happens when you marry a thug," they said. Priscilla couldn't take their insults anymore. Not after she had defended me so vehemently when we got married. "Like father, like son," the DA told her. I wished he had said it to my face. I was not a thug and sure as heck was not like Daddy. I would never be like him. Whenever his spirit wanted to come out of me, I pushed it back. Even James was blaming me for what transpired between me and the officer.

"*Us* brothers have to keep a cool head in these situations," he told me.

"Brothers!"

He was a cool guy. But we obviously grew up in two different worlds. While his parents were preparing him for Ivy League law school, I was trying to protect Mamma from Daddy's fists. We were brothers all right—comrades with different roots. I wondered how he would have turned out, growing up in a hollow hell like I did. We may have sat next to each other in class, but we weren't the same. I had to fight harder to get to where I was.

"I'm not above the fray of racism," James noted. "But brother," he said, "We've come a long way. No more excuses. You could've handled things better and not be so prone to anger."

He didn't think race had anything to do with the cop shooting me. It might have been so, but once someone has suffered injustice, even the hand that is meant to protect and serve falls prey to cynicism. I was getting tired of being looked upon as the offender. And yet, still be the one feeling the sting. The officer showed remorse. "I'm sorry," he told Priscilla. Surely, he felt some pain. And now, I hated me. A criminal, and hotheaded fool in the eyes of whom I wed. A brother I once looked up to had me doubting my own hands. Priscilla hadn't lied. Sometimes the verdict comes before the indictment. And once you're accused, the stench may never leave. She had forsworn her own ruling. I had a bullet put into me because the ghost of my childhood horror had come back to haunt me. I tried to keep myself together as best I could, listening to Priscilla's distressing sob. "There are other ways you know, you could've vented your anger," she said.

"I'm so sorry you feel this way," I told her, slightly holding on to my breath. I was getting sick of her, tired of her making me out to be the fall guy. "How do I know that you're not sleeping with some of these men when you stay out late?" I told her.

She clobbered me with her fist.

"Know who you're talking to. I'm not one of those stupid tramps you've been with," she hollered.

I was hoping she wasn't referring to Nadine. Priscilla's discontentment was far from over.

"How could you do this to me?" She continued her frantic rant, rattling my nerves all the more.

"I've been humiliated, all because you can't control your temper," she let loose her resentment.

"So, now I'm a disgrace?" I glanced at her, all the while thinking it was my spiteful reward for marrying her.

"Go ahead, say it, we're all the same. Say it damn it! After I've loved you more than I ever thought I could," her voice rising like thunder.

Was she serious? She had lied to me. And James was an accomplice. Spending most nights out drinking at a bar is not what a good wife does, I told her. Especially when her husband desperately needs her. I could tell by the look on her face how disappointed she was. Her bedroom eyes had lost their summer heat.

"You need to grow up, Violin," she raised both hands angrily to her face and put her head down.

I had grown, otherwise my hands would already be guilty of slaughter.

"What did you think, Priscilla?" I asked. "What did you think it was going to be like when you chose to marry pain?" She was bringing more carnage to an already frail heart. "I have had this thing inside of me," I told Priscilla. "It's been eating me alive. My bones may be covered with flesh, but I might as well be dead. It's because of you, I ain't dead yet. You have kept me alive, Priscilla, but now I feel betrayed," I slowly withdrew my hand, about to hold her chin.

"Doom me to hell then, for not knowing how to handle this," she grabbed her purse, about to leave me stranded, drowning in my own man-child rage.

I took hold of her; my knees yielding under the weight of my demented spirit. "I love you, that's about the only thing I'm sure of," I pulled her towards me. Lust burned within me like rum fire. Tears of longing welled up, though she had given me grief. Hurt, mad as hell, yet wanting peace, and desperate for her to love me.

"Please, don't walk out on me," I begged her. My face pinned against hers. "Just answer this," I asked, "Do you still love me?"

She nodded. Her breasts, warm and reassuring against my heartbeat. "Viol..." she started to utter my name.

"Please, not a word," I placed my hand over her lips.

"You mean the world to me," I told her.

I could breathe again. I learned, once you've captured a man's heart, you will have it for life. Priscilla had ensnared mine. I had been angry, thinking she was heartbroken, having married me. She had spent weeks, crying. Endless nights, sobbing at a bar, afraid of losing her mind. She didn't know how to tell me. She even thought about resigning her position at the office. The self-loathing pity and hate coming out of me was like a slap in the face.

"I've lost my voice, arguing with so-called friends, about how much of a good man you are," she said.

The first time I laid eyes on Priscilla, something in me shook. It scared me to death. I fought it, understanding all too well the world we lived in. We joined hands, nonetheless, to become one. One heart, one love, but still found ourselves worlds apart. I finally had to let go. "There's so much about me I'm afraid that can't be loved," I told her. No one had ever warmed my heart in such a way, apart from Nadine.

"We need to get past this. No more, from now on, no more talks about why I married you, or what anyone thinks of you. I love you as you are," she said.

I wondered how long she would continue to love the madness in me.

CHAPTER TEN

No longer on probation, I was a free man again. Although not as free as I had been before justice decreed me to be a criminal. "You're far from that," Priscilla told me. I still felt like an outlaw. Always looking over my shoulders. The law granted me freedom. And yet, my feet seemed bound by link chains. I felt like a wild beast tied to a street pole. There was a world of opportunity surrounding me. I was stuck watching everyone laugh and dance, as if they were mocking me. My own sin held me captive of its unforgiving hands. I was beginning to despise who I had become. I would still be able to go to law school. Priscilla promised to help me get out of the hole I had dug myself into. I told her if my moral standing was not good enough for broken justice, then my freedom was in vain. She told me not to look too far ahead. I still had a year or two to go before starting law school. It seemed like an eternity. While the judge had instructed me to stay in school, some administrators didn't seem to want me in their lecturing halls. They didn't say it, then again, they didn't have to. I did not do well in school while on probation. "You must be a first-time offender," one of the administrators had asked. I figured it must have been how fate had intended the world to be. Each one trapped inside of his or her own box. Some are in it because it will be their home until they die. Others are caged in, through no fault of their own. I still felt the sting of Daddy's wrath.

Mamma's wounds lingered like a cut from a knife blade. My soul was going through war against my own rage. Knowing what to do, having someone show you, and still not being able to do it was my harsh reality. I could no longer stomach it. My mind had enough of the battle. Voices in my head, singing to me every day; the struggle was hopeless. I saw Mamma's ghost everywhere. Some wore it well. While others, as stealthily as they may have tried, couldn't dress up their wounds. They all had Mamma's spirit. Most of the time, I wasn't wrong. My senses would rev up in an instant around these women. At a bar one night, while having a few drinks with Priscilla, my heart shot up, the moment the waitress came to our table. She greeted us with a smile. I saw much more than a cheerful grin. She was extremely beautiful, with skin the color of caramelized sugar. She had a maroon shawl over her head, looking very much like an African queen. I watched her, and whether she knew it or not, our spirits connected. Priscilla was a tad bit jealous.

"Why do you look at her that way," she asked.

I sensed a troubled spirit underneath the layer of her imposing beauty.

"Where is your accent from?" Priscilla asked, when she returned to our table.

She said she was from the Ivory Coast.

"Ah bon, vous parlez donc Francais?" (So, you speak French then,) I asked.

"Oui," she replied, seemingly downcast.

"Tu habites loin d'ici?" (Do you live far from here) she asked.

I told her, we lived only a couple of miles away. She said she had been working three jobs to help support her son.

"Are you married?" I asked?"

Her cheeks drew-out, about to offer another beautiful smile. But then, she broke down crying.

"My life is a mess," she said, her voice quivering.

Tilting her body to hand us our drinks, she dropped the serving dish when she noticed me staring at her neck. There was a large welt along her neckline.

"Who did this to you?" I asked.

She collapsed on our table. I was trying to turn her over, rolling her shirt back to cover her rear. There were colorful ridges all over her body. "Oh my God, that's terrible," Priscilla cried out. "Whoever did this to her should go to Hell," she said.

As if trying to recover from another bad dream in my nightmarish life wasn't daunting enough, Priscilla started to question my increasing lack of passion. She said it was more than simply losing interest in the bedroom. She sensed me pulling away. I hated doing it; sharing my love with other women. But how do you run from what so desperately wants to snare you. How do you unlove what can make you whole again? Whatever I had left in me was now the joy of other women. They didn't come looking for love. I gave it to them. I couldn't help it. I couldn't stop thinking about these women. Women like Lucille. She was standing at the bus stop, after I had picked up Priscilla at the courthouse. I pulled over, driving past her. "Watch what happens," I told Priscilla. "Violin, you're starting to scare me. You've taken it too far," she said. I had met Lucille one Sunday morning at the grocery store. She was a stunningly attractive Black woman. "Look! You see this woman, I can tell she's hurting," I told Priscilla. It was just something about her. Not a moment too soon, the same round looking fella who stood behind her like a bodyguard at the grocery store pulled up. He snatched her hair as soon as she'd stepped foot in the car. I had seen him doing it quite a few times, and even worse. There had been a hand to the face, a slap on the head, and almost a chokehold. He didn't introduce himself at the grocery store. I saw the fear in Lucille's eyes, standing next to him. Before long, I had looked for Lucille and offered her a taste of my love.

"You need to mind your own business and make sure your wife is happy," Priscilla had said. The emotional roller coaster had taken me on a ride from curiosity to pity—from pity—to utter disgust—from repulsion to another woman's bed. It felt like love. Though I knew it wasn't. My mind had fallen prey to so many of these women. It was the same with Ms. Brookline; the teacher who lived in our building. My heart did beat like rapid fire for her. But I heard them, she and her husband, after he nearly took her life that night. It sounded as if he was pounding her flesh again. This time, she was enjoying it. They were so loud, I could hear them even after covering my ears with a pillow. The ceiling started shaking. Well good for her then, I thought. I was so angry. I hated Ms. Brookline. Mamma often did the same thing.

Priscilla and I started spending most nights out in the city. She thought it would bring us closer. Sometimes, there is no reality in what the night conveys. I conceded. Priscilla loved the glitz of New York City. I found no pleasure in it. I was becoming too temperamental, she said. And so, it shouldn't have been a surprise when I told her the night life wasn't for us anymore. There was too much drinking with friends, not my friends, but hers. "Well-to-do connections," she called them, who would help advance her career. But all they seemed to want was to get in her pants. I didn't care if it was for a good cause. Most of these men showed up with their trophy wives. And yet, I saw the way they looked at Priscilla. One of them, Jerry, who owned several high-end retail chains, and his own private jet, told Priscilla he would love to take her home. She said it was a foolish joke from an old friend. His wife didn't think it was funny. Neither did I. Yet Priscilla appeared to relish these decadent advances. Perhaps hoping it would revive my dwindling passion. Being in the company of these wealthy, older men, I felt like a menial inner-city boy. An empty vessel without a voice, even. Their senseless jokes weren't all that amusing. Had they all been White men, I wouldn't have felt so grim. In my warped mind, most White men had grown up with heavy spoons of privilege. The men who sat at our round table looked like me. Many of whom were at one time urban Black kids who had hustled their way out of the hood. It felt worse, being upstaged by them. I wondered if Priscilla secretly wished she had married one of them.

I withdrew into a shell. The beat of the drum, I could no longer escape. The world closing in on me. Life was stringing me through the needle. "Enough! Why can't we go out? Why can't we be happy?" Priscilla groaned. She was losing her patience with me. She said I was living life, always afraid. She couldn't take it anymore. The voices got louder. They no longer sounded like soft rain. *"Violine is dead. You've had the fun years. You thought you were a woman's man. But now you're on your way to hell."* I would hear the front door opening in my sleep. The keys ringing like a buzzer before another round of a boxing match. My heart began to race, throbbing like fighting drums. I was always too young to referee the bouts. The bluish-purple lumps on Mamma's face told me who got knocked out. Her cries had upended my world. "I think it's best if I walk away," I told Priscilla. A real man learns when to run. She said I needed help. "With what?" I told her.

When shame engulfs you, hush takes on its face. The colors you bleed; the world can't see. "What color is your skin?" Mamma would ask. "Black, like midnight darkness," I would answer. "Wear it like a king," she said, though the world didn't see me that way. "I feel like I'm losing my mind, sweetie. But I can't leave you here. I have to push, laugh, and pretend everything is well," Mamma said. I felt so miserable, listening to her visceral cry. Just like Daddy, Mamma used to be a schoolteacher back home. She was always proud that she had helped raise young minds. She had nurtured them to be kings and queens. To stand tall against the plague of self-contempt. My struggles were far beyond the neglect of self-worth. A wicked wind had found its way inside of me. And if evil had entered a man, Mamma said, he had to change course real fast, to rid himself of its sinful grip. My solitude became my escape. Like a cocoon, it was where I could dress up the beast. Priscilla was losing touch with my reality.

My kids didn't see me much anymore. Whatever in me waiting to explode, I kept far from them. Still lost in broken women, old habits streamed back to life like wine dimming my soul. Some sins fight you harder than others. As much as I tried, my will to keep them at bay was only assuaged by a relentless rage. I was in love with Priscilla. The darkness inside of me had fallen out of love. "Why stay married then, if you're no longer attracted to me?" she asked. She said she had an array of men begging to be with her. I came close to hitting her. I couldn't, afraid of what my hands would do to her. Priscilla never had a clue. Perhaps she did want the fury to come out of me. She always said it was best to let out frustration. Healing comes from letting go, she said. How was I going to be healed by punishing the one I love? Granted, with me sharing myself with other women while neglecting my wife, she was already exhausted. Trying to remain faithful, I wanted to crush her bones. I fought like hell to keep sane. I didn't know whom or what I was fighting. But it was there, day and night, tugging at me, singing to me. I had struggled far too long. No matter what I did to cast away the beast, it always found its way home. I was afraid the world would see what my own heart despised in me.

How do you tell someone you love everything about your soul? You only explain what you think they see; when your mind is not right. I longed for someone to talk to. Most friends acted like foes in days of trouble. And sometimes, a friend is left without a choice. Who can you talk to? They'll run, too weak, or petrified to help you carry your burden. Priscilla thought it was insane of me to think that way. Back in high school, Nadine and Ernest, a cousin of Josie's boyfriend were the only ones I would let in. They

174

operated like an army. They always had my back. Ernest and I fell off. He took me to see his girlfriend one day after school. As soon as we got to her house, he kicked her in the jaw. She started to cry, telling him how much it hurt. "See, that's how you treat a tramp," he said. He was upset she had been too friendly with a boy at school. Ernest and I never once spoke again. I left his girlfriend's home that day, feeling very much like a coward. At first, I thought his girlfriend's parents were home, hearing a muffled sound coming from another room. It was the girl's brother-in-law in the house. He was the true coward. When he finally came out, he shook Ernest's hand and told the girl to keep quiet. I found out later, he had also been thumping on his girlfriend. They both, I thought, needed to be condemned to Hell. Then again, Ernest was a good kid. He was a good friend before I saw him hitting his girlfriend. He would have given me the shirt off his back if asked. But what he did was disgraceful. I had seen Daddy do the same thing countless times. It was like a sickness, a disgusting bug. Perhaps, the one who watched and did not say anything was just as revolting.

Struggling to win over demons comes at a cost. My shell had a lot of secrets buried inside. It was silly of me to think that life with Priscilla would be a fairytale. Nothing would ever be. Not in my deranged life. I found a new friend. Rosa, the stripper at the club, Downtown Brooklyn. She kept me from being utterly out of my mind. Rosa understood the world Priscilla didn't know existed in me. "Why the sad face? cheer up," She intoned when we first met. We were having a drink behind the bar, where devils meet. I told her there was no need to charm me. "I'm already yours," I said. She paused, then offered me a dance which turned my legs weak. Though we could only meet behind closed doors, Rosa became a good friend. When she was eight years old, after she had come home from school, Rosa saw her mother's body lifeless in a pool of blood. Her father did it. Her mother's eyes were like the dark moon, she said. While she was only a child when it happened, it had been carved in her memory. She had been going through fifteen years of hell ever since that day. Priscilla had only witnessed such anguish as an outsider looking in. Inside that world, love and misery are the same. They have no middle. The heart who loves, also hates. Survival of self takes place one breath at a time. The wounds are not always obvious. And I doubt they will ever be. "I wear my scars in my heart," Rosa told me. A callous heart was her only defense, she said. She frequently wore dark clothing. Mostly black, from morning until the cover of night. Then, she came out. The beauty of an embattled "Boricua" princess. I told her, she was even more captivating under the dark veil. She wanted to run.

"That part of me, I only share with closed heart," she said. She already did when our lips touched.

Who but Rosa could understand the world I was living in? My heart wasn't cold. At home, I was becoming submissive to Priscilla. It was out of fear I would hurt her one day. Everything she wanted, I gave. Apart from me. It turned her off. No man denies his wife love. It is sacrilegious, more ungodly than chasing after deserted brides. Priscilla had been trying to find a cure. There were times when I would get so irritated; I started breaking things around the house. Priscilla hadn't done anything wrong. I was angry with myself for what I wasn't able to give. Perhaps, incensed at humanity as well for what it was doing to me. At first, Priscilla pretended not to notice. Something awful was happening. Like when you're living a lie, but reality keeps coming back to smack you in the face. Everything I did was met with repulsion. Then, it got really bad. "There are doctors who can help you; if not, we're getting a divorce," Priscilla lastly blurted out, her frost draping over me. It was going to take more than her grief to convince me a shrink could help solve my angst. Mamma once told me, she took medications, which almost made her go crazy. She'd told the doctor that she was depressed. Whatever he gave her almost turned Mamma into a monster. Some nights, I saw her talking to herself. It scared me. "What's wrong,

Mamma," I asked. She said she felt like hitting people at work. One day, while she and I were on the bus after seeing the doctor, everyone started to stare at her as though she was out of her mind. Mamma was making loud noises and talking to herself. This woman who sat next to us said she felt sorry for me. There were a bunch of kids on the bus who started laughing. Lord knows I wanted to hurt them. Mamma told me to forgive them. Little did she realize; some people at her church did the same thing. They would sit far from her. Others would laugh, just like the kids on the bus had done. "No way," I didn't want any help, I told Priscilla. My sickness had no cure.

On our way to a dinner party, evil came to conquer me. It relentlessly pressed against my chest, towering its strength over my abdomen. I was yet again angry without a cause. Priscilla looked dizzyingly glorious that night. She had on a pierced, black lace dress, with her golden hair pulled back. The dress had been a surprise, which I got her a few weeks after we started dating. I now hated it. As soon as we had stepped foot inside the restaurant, it suddenly dawned on me why I may have been filled with so much rage. I was once again in the company of incredibly snobbish men. Most of them, undoubtedly lusting after my wife. I had vowed to stop attending these pretentious events. Priscilla told me it was nothing more than a surprise farewell to a colleague who was moving to Costa Rica. James did not attend. He ditched the occasion for a trip out of town with his future bride. I was relieved he was not around. Answering the same questions over and over again, about why I hadn't studied law like he had was starting to get tiring. Everyone appeared to be staring me down, as though I was beneath them. Priscilla thought I was acting paranoid. Perhaps I was. But what did not being right in the head had to do with married men coveting my wife. I didn't like the way her fine-looking blue eyes flirted with these men. They were like swayed jewels. Like sapphire waiting to be embezzled. These men assuredly saw in Priscilla what had also gotten me engrossed. She was extremely pleasant and overly friendly with them. She called it her "Innate charm." I told her, it would one day get her in trouble with unscrupulous men, never intended for her own husband to be the victim of her scheming charm.

What began as an unwelcoming going away party almost turned into a lovers' bloodbath, after Eric walked in. He and Priscilla had once dated while in law school. He was tall, fair skinned, and had hazel green eyes. I sensed something was wrong the moment he sat next to Priscilla. He stared at her for so long, as if he were undressing her with his eyes. When Priscilla saw him, her eyes lit up. They hadn't gazed at me that way in quite a long time. "Eric!" she moaned at his gallant entrance, nearly falling out of her chair. She was acting like a schoolgirl, seeing her first crush. "It's been a long time; I didn't know you were invited," she said.

So lost in his aura, she forgot to introduce me as her husband. Sweat started pouring out of her, as if the room was like a sauna. Eric took out the handkerchief buried underneath his jacket and dabbed her face. "You're still beautiful," he gathered his lips. Priscilla couldn't stop smiling. Her face turned red, flushed with exhilaration. My teeth began to gnash uncontrollably. Finally! She thought of her husband. "Oh my God, I am so sorry," she said. I was the laughingstock at the table.

Few words were spoken in the car. With Priscilla's unnerving silence, and my own hush of tunnel vision, everything seemed meaningless. "I hate that this is happening," she mumbled to herself. The damage was already done. When we got to the house, I grabbed a bottle of Cognac and nearly swallowed all of it. I had done worse. The worst thing a man could do to his wife. It felt as if Priscilla had committed a greater sin. I could feel her stab wounds all over my chest. And yet, I wanted her more than ever. I chased after Priscilla with pain, with love, and thirst of a resentful lover. "I'm weak from you loving me," she said, exhaling long breaths. We made up; yet I longed for something more—a sick love. The kind that likes to crash and burn. I was in need of it. "I have to go clear my head," I told Priscilla. She was baffled by my unsentimental escape.

"That's very cold-hearted of you, after making love to me," she said.

I was a wretched soul. One, no one would envy. And yet, Priscilla had made it her home. The sweet butterfly Mamma talked about truly loved me. Evil deeds, however, are not always curbed by love. Rosa knew how to quench my lonely craving. I had to go find her. The voices gleaned with flashes of light.

I got to Rosa's house, and soon after she had opened the door, my soul was uncovered. "What's wrong, baby?" She asked. I didn't want to touch her. A wave of heavy guilt ripping my heart apart. It brought tears to Rosa's eyes. Not because I had changed my mind. It was what I then said to her that made her tears dropped. "We're both sick people," I told her. Our intimate affair was like a bandage. We tried to cover years of emotional anguish with angry sex. It was to no end. It was our way of covering up the pain. It had no substance. We were two empty vessels, trying to appease our longings with a perverse affection. A sick love, which real love had failed to cure. "I love you,"

Rosa smashed my lips with a kiss. She wanted me to go home to my wife. For the first time in my life, the mirror showed me how twisted my mind had become. My soul bitter.

After leaving Rosa's house, walking to my car, I noticed a black truck across the street. It looked similar to Priscilla's car. I felt on edge, thinking, there was no way Priscilla had followed me. After opening my car door, glancing at the rear-view mirror, I saw Priscilla's angry stare in the back seat. My heart pounded with haste. She took off her shoes, and launched them at me, striking me in the back of the head. She then crouched over and began punching me with a hail of closed fists.

"You disgusting pig," she kept screaming, relentless in pounding my head, and using her fingers as if driving nails through me. She left more than thumbprints on my neck. I could feel the wet sting of her fingernails. I ran out of the car, telling her, I was just visiting a friend. She continued her persistent assault, following me out onto the street. When her ambush finally ended, I held her in my arms. "I'm sorry, I'm a sick man," I told her. She struck my chest with her fist. The heels of her shoe left a huge cut on my face. Her tears left me speechless. The embarrassment of having snooping neighbors watching me get beaten down seemed worse than an open wound.

I confessed to Priscilla, telling her what I had been doing. She still couldn't grasp the perversity of my sick world. She thought the demons had turned me into an addict. If it were so, I told her, she would have been the one held captive. It was more than simply dissolute urges. War raging inside my head, there was a torrent of bottled-up pain and anger burning within me. Priscilla thought my emotional pain had perhaps triggered a mental illness. I knew my mind wasn't right. But if I was mentally unstable, I asked, what did Daddy suffer from? I finally agreed to get help. I was getting tired of the emotional roller coaster. At the hospital that same week, they were bringing a body in, a young girl. I nudged over to see who it was. My heart nearly sank to the ground. It was Rosa. She was in bad shape. The doctors tried all they could, but they couldn't revive her. She died; Rosa died of a drug overdose. She was only twenty-four years old. I should have known this was going to happen. When I left her that night, Rosa told me something foreshadowing her withdrawal to the grave. "See you in Hell," she said, "that's where we both belong." She said it with a smile, but thinking back, her cold grin may have been a cry for help. My hands were stained with her blood, smeared with guilt. I might as well had been the one who shot her up with the needle. It fired off the pain right into her heart. I missed being with Rosa. She was a good friend. She once told me, friends shouldn't let friends slip away. I did. I cried until my eyes had only dried tears. Seeing her lifeless body, I was familiar with that picture. I had seen it every day. It prompted me to think, what kind of life is this that pays so dearly.

That night, I heard the chiming of church bells. Not the ones that had been talking and singing to me. But old friends. I hadn't heard them since Mamma died. With a host of shadowy figures inside my head, Priscilla was right, I needed help. "If there is a way back, take me there. Take me back into Mamma's stomach," I mourned. I was never without torment, nor did I have relief since leaving her womb. I was never free from this thing inside of me. Back home, I once cracked a beer bottle on Jessy's head for teasing me. My grandmother was so upset. She chastised me for hours and had me kneel on top of the graveled floor. She whipped me at least a dozen times. Far more than she ever had with her *martinet*– the wooden stick with more than a dozen leather straps at the edge. The additional lashes, I thought, were because I had wasted the castor oil she had poured into the bottle. But, "you're too damn good of a child to do something like this," she said. Mamma never said anything. She just sat there, watching me getting beat like an untamed mule. But then, she had tears in her eyes. Mamma didn't like using the *martinet*. Her tongue was her rod. She had a way of making me feel so much shame about whatever I had done wrong. Sometimes, I wished she had instead used her hands or even a belt to raise me upright. Her words hurt just as much as the welts left on my skin. It didn't matter. Whipping, shaming, they felt the same. When I had to carry my wet mattress out to dry in the sun for everyone to see, they all would make fun of me. It was then, hell began to visit me. My mind took me places I couldn't even tell Mamma about. I would hear loud voices in my head. I tried to ignore them, crying for them to leave. More of them moved in. They came in droves, bringing with them, sweet sounds of trumpets and violins. They were never to be talked about. Never to be heard by anybody else. I didn't always remember everything. There were a lot of things perhaps, I had been too afraid to recall. They would always remind me—my invisible friends. They kept me safe at night. They wouldn't tell me their names. Yet I recalled each one by their melody. When they all would visit at once, the song went on all night. One after another, their symphony would play in my head. I could no longer castoff what had kept me alive. What had kept me smiling; feeling the world was ashamed of me breathing its air. They were more than friends, even more than the ones who claimed to love me. They were me.

CHAPTER ELEVEN

Priscilla held my hands. "It's okay honey; tell him what's been going on with you," staring down the district attorney. He was snooping to find out how I had been doing. "Joe, there are many like me in the system. You see our wounds and you think we're monsters. But we're not. Our souls indeed are filled with demons. But even with our evil deeds, our hearts are not as heinous as most would like to believe. Many of us didn't suddenly wake up one day and sought to commit acts that were beyond the pale. The spirit of fear, hurt, and abandonment found us. We didn't volunteer for our minds to be their home. Some of us are teachers, doctors, and even lawyers." He laughed. "We're fathers, daughters, and sons. We're sisters, and mothers."

The DA said it was nothing but a sorry excuse when I told him about my unspeakable nightmares. I wondered where he would have ended up if he grew up breathing the lake of fire like I did. If he were raised with a volley of fists up his nose or a hail of kicks under his ribs. Worst, what if the blood of the one who nursed him ran through his heart like burning coal. Would he then be able to stand tall enough to speak?

We've all been through something, some, even in this hell. I gather most of them have. Until I tell them how it felt watching Mamma die a slow death. It was like looking down the barrel of a gun. Each time the trigger is pulled, you worry it may be your last breath. You lose faith, without ever having hope. When you lose your dignity young, you die young. The rest of your life is spent chasing the shadow of what used to be. Hopeless, and with no one to help, I blamed Mamma sometimes. Then again, it wasn't her fault. And Daddy, well, I know now the horrifying demons he had to battle. Even after putting them to sleep, they come back to torment like seven serpents of Hell. They handed me the keys to a wretched life, a warped mind, then helped me dig my own grave. Priscilla was dead-on. I needed help. Help sometimes, doesn't come soon enough.

The days were filled with joy, growing up back home. The sun, bright like beams of light from heaven. The middle of the day was like a carnival. But at night was when the demons came. At night was when I cringed in fear for you. At night was when I cried for you. At night was when I worried. At night was when my head pounded for you. At night was when I wondered if I would ever see you again. The night I wanted to come to you, I wondered if you were still breathing.

"Here, take this, it's from Jessy," Priscilla handed me a Bible with a note, after I had laid down the pen. Jessy had found God. And Josie, he said, was doing well. He promised to visit, soon. The best the DA would offer is to spare my life. Priscilla vowed to challenge any presumption of guilt with an insanity plea. Either way, I wouldn't be free. Hell is hell, regardless if it burns fast or slow. "How did I end up here? I'm scared, I'm scared, baby. I can't even sleep at night," I cried out to Priscilla. It all started that night, that foggy winter night on my way to hell.

"Hurry! Please, come now," Noelle, sounding very much in fear for her own life shouted. It was the same day Priscilla made an appointment for me to see a shrink. Bob was beating on Nadine again. The bedroom door was locked, but Noelle could hear the loud thumps and her mother's frantic screams. She thought Nadine was being thrown against the wall. Bob told her not to worry or call the police. The thunderous blows could not remain silent behind Nadine's groaning. "Mommy sounds like she's dying in there," Noelle cried out. Her voice quaking with intense fear. "Please hurry, he's going to kill her," she screeched out once again. Priscilla wasn't home. I didn't even bother to call her. It was going to be a bloody date with fate. I didn't want her hands tainted in any way. Driving up to Long Island, my mind had nothing but rage fueling its thirst. It reminded me of the last time I sat behind the wheel with so much fury in me. A heart filled with so much despair has no regrets. The law wasn't kind to me then and surely would not grant me justice this time around. I wanted to kill Bob. As if fate had hastened the road to hell, I took so many red lights without once being stopped by the police. Then again, it may have been because of the fog. It was brutal along the long-stretched roads. This weird song then started playing in my head. Its tune was one of hate, and its rhythm, made up of uninhibited rage. The drums, then thumped louder. The concerto wailing over the bow and strings, the closer I had gotten to Nadine's house. Passing by a car on the side of the road, its interior lights dimmed, as a massive tree limb had crumbled its rooftop. I said a prayer and yet could not stop. There was then this slight breeze moving through me. It felt like the rift of a guilty conscience. The swirl of its evil wind inside of me, the boundary of the abyss was not far from my errant flesh. The song grew louder, going through the steel fences. The scorching fury inside my head had led me to the gates of hell. I was like a wrecked ship, departing the shore, about to sail into the depths of the ocean. I entered the room quietly, after Nya and Noelle had let me in. Nadine lay on her stomach, with Sarah lying next to her. They both looked sound asleep, Sarah's head resting on her mother's back. I told my twin daughters to go in their rooms and not to come out.

"What are you about to do?" Nya asked.

"Go to your room," I told her.

"Mommy said Bob felt bad about what he did," she said.

"GO TO YOUR ROOM!" I yelled at her, hearing my teeth gnashing. Both she and her sister ran.

"Daddy, you're scaring us," they said. They must have seen the evil in my eyes. Bob was in another room, Noelle told me. I felt a strange sensation. My anger rose like the sear of a sea monster. And yet, I felt the fright of a lonesome little boy.

"No! Stop me from doing this." They wouldn't' answer. The melody egging me on. Looking out the skylight above the faintly lit hall, before propping the door open, I saw a hand amidst the fog. It was dark in color. There was a large print written on its palm, with the words "LIVE, BOB." My eyes could've fooled me. My hands began to shake. The little boy had lost the struggle. I wasn't brave enough the day Mamma died. I had let her down.

It must have truly come as a thief in the night. Death always sneaks up on you, Mamma said. One crushing blow to the neck after I had entered the room; his body jerked and went limp. The light then brightly shining, uncovering my sin.

"Oh my God, what have you done?" Nadine shouted with a mouthful of terror.

She ran to Bob. He didn't have any breath left.

"I did it for you," I said. My high school sweetheart all bruised up, her face looking as if it had been a punching bag.

"I did it for you," I opened my arms for her to come to me, still holding the bloody knife.

"Oh my goodness! You're a sick man; what have you done to my husband?" Nadine kept yelling, crouching over Bob, her hands shaky. She looked confused and in shock, covering his wound with the blood-soaked pillow. "Bob, Bob! Baby, please wake up," her voice dipping and her eyes raining tears.

"Baby? Is she serious? I tried to speak, but the words wouldn't come out.

"He's a monster," I shouted, hoping she would come to me.

"No, Violin, you are. You're the one holding the knife," she yelled back, her cry reverberating inside of me. "I can't believe this is happening. I have to call an ambulance. I'm calling the police," she said. I wanted to end it all. I felt betrayed. The room started spinning. Mamma was standing near the edge of the bed. Her eyes covered with a black cloth. It was to hide my terrible sin, the men in white robes standing at her side uttered. One of them had a huge gavel thrusted in midair, about to sentence me to death. "Your hell is not yet over," he said.

I had taken another man's life. I sent him to the grave with the symphony of my twisted soul. Yielding my humanity to the sword, my life lost in my insanity. Who I was, had been lost, avenging love. I was just like Daddy, even worse. "I did it for you," I kept crying out to Nadine.

"You need help, Violin; you're all screwed up," she said.

My daughters looked on, as the officers were taking me away. Noelle and Nya were crying. But Sarah, my baby girl, started clapping. It tore my heart apart.

"State your name?" the officer asked.

"Violin, my name is Violin, the son of Violine," I answered.

I'm locked up behind bars. I'm a criminal—hated by everyone. In the military, a purple heart is given to soldiers killed or wounded in combat. What is my reward? A purple heart, given to me by years of pretending and fighting demons. They wounded me. They killed my soul. What is my reward? "The dragon's dungeon?" Am I celebrated? Underneath my smile, although there aren't any smiles anymore, is still a scared little boy in a grown man's body. I've fought against everything that came at me like a soldier. I've taken every bullet in warfare. What is my reward? "Oh my God! What has happened to me?" Maybe it has to do with the small chime box Mamma gave me when I was a little boy. "It will put you to sleep and get rid of all your bad dreams," she said. She gave it to me after I told her I had heard a monster in her bedroom. The chime box used to keep me safe at night. I broke it in half. I gave one half to Mamma and the other half to Daddy; so they could have sweet dreams and keep the monster from coming back. I didn't need it anymore. I had new friends.

December 25th, 2010

My name is Violin; I'm the son the world does not know about.

Author's Note

Not long after the publication of this novel, two friends lost their lives, defending a woman from domestic abuse. This work of fiction serves to memorialize their selfless act of valor. Some have deemed this novel a tough read. While the story has its moments of laughter, and episodes of innocence, rooted in youthful passion, it is, nonetheless, a reflection of the horrid impact of both domestic abuse and mental illness. It is my hope that this novel will foster more dialogue and awareness about these silent plagues.